Dear Reader,

As I began work on *Plain Jane's Prince Charming,*
I couldn't stop thinking about a little girl in my son's
preschool class who had been diagnosed with acute
lymphoblastic leukemia (ALL). While her family
navigated their way through an overwhelming new
world of oncology, treatment protocols and hospitals,
the children in the preschool made a hand-print quilt
for their classmate and waited for her return. Friends
sought ways to help—bringing meals, praying and
helping with her sister, who was in kindergarten.

Thankfully, her leukemia went into remission and
she returned to preschool, but her chemotherapy
treatments continued. Eager to help others, her
parents organized a local benefit for The Leukemia
& Lymphoma Society.

I was so moved by the courage of this family, and
the love and support that flowed from their friends
and the community, that they all wove their way
into the backdrop of this story. Leukemia is a
horrible disease, but it's not without hope. And
that's what I wanted to show in this romance—
hope, heart and a happily-ever-after.

Melissa McClone

P.S. If you would like to learn more about
ALL, or how you can help, please visit
The Leukemia & Lymphoma Society
Web site at www.leukemia-lymphoma.org

MELISSA MCCLONE

With a degree in mechanical engineering from Stanford University, the last thing Melissa McClone ever thought she would be doing was writing romance novels. But analyzing engines for a major U.S. airline just couldn't compete with her "happily-ever-afters."

When she isn't writing, caring for her three young children or doing laundry, Melissa loves to curl up on the couch with a cup of tea, her cats and a good book. She enjoys watching home decorating shows to get ideas for her house—a 1939 cottage that is *slowly* being renovated. Melissa lives in Lake Oswego, Oregon, with her own real-life hero husband, two daughters, a son, two lovable but oh-so-spoiled indoor cats and a no-longer-stray outdoor kitty that decided to call the garage home. Melissa loves to hear from her readers. You can write to her at P.O. Box 63, Lake Oswego, OR 97034, U.S.A.

Plain Jane's
Prince
Charming

MELISSA
McCLONE

SILHOUETTE *Romance*®
Published by Silhouette Books
America's Publisher of Contemporary Romance

 SILHOUETTE BOOKS

ISBN-13: 978-0-373-19838-2
ISBN-10: 0-373-19838-8

PLAIN JANE'S PRINCE CHARMING

Copyright © 2006 by Melissa McClone

First North American Publication 2006

Visit Silhouette Books at www.eHarlequin.com

Printed in U.S.A.

Melissa McClone on *Plain Jane's Prince Charming:*

"I raided my own wardrobe to dress my heroine Jane. Her red field coat, black long-sleeved T-shirt and tan corduroy pants came from my closet. I used to wear purple wire-rimmed eyeglasses, too, until one of my children broke the frames. Let's hope Jane has better luck with hers!"

Don't miss Melissa's next heartwarming story,

Marriage for Baby, (#3947)

coming in April 2006,
only from Harlequin Romance®

For Taylor Jackson

CHAPTER ONE

"MR. RYDER." Standing in the foyer of Cyberworx's state-of-the-art meeting facility, Jane Dawson couldn't believe how steady her voice sounded when inside she felt like a coffee bean being ground into tiny bits. Still she managed to smile at the gray-haired businessman. "I would like to speak with you. For a minute. That is if you have time. Please."

Jane winced.

So much for being smooth and collected, but this was different from speaking with customers while she managed the Hearth, a trendy coffee house in downtown Portland, Oregon. That job required patience, a smile and making sure the staff at the counter got the orders right, not cultured eloquence and grace.

"You want to speak to me?" In spite of his tailored suit, he looked more like a doting grandfather than the successful CEO of a multinational hi-tech company. "Chase… Ryder?"

He sounded surprised.

Of course, he did. People like Jane, college drop-outs who brewed coffee all day, didn't usually approach people like him. And normally she wouldn't. Especially when picking up after a catering job. On her day off.

But this wasn't a normal situation.

She'd jumped at the chance to set up and pick up the breakfast meeting buffet for thirty guests at the corporate headquarters though catering jobs weren't her usual responsibility. Her boss, Zoe, had offered her the opportunity to meet Chase Ryder, and Jane wasn't going to blow it.

Act like you know what you're doing. Saying. And think before you open your mouth. Zoe's advice echoed in Jane's head. She raised her chin. "Yes, I would, Mr. Ryder."

His grin deepened the lines around his mouth and eyes. "I'm more than happy to speak with you, miss."

Jane hadn't felt this light, this hopeful in…well, years.

"Unfortunately," he continued, "I'm not Chase Ryder."

Her heart plummeted to her feet, as if two fifty-pound bags of Sumatra Gayo Mountain coffee beans had been dumped on each of her shoulders.

Not Chase Ryder.

How could she have made such a big mistake? Her assistant manager, Ally, had told Jane she couldn't miss the Cyberworx's head honcho. Tall, handsome and surrounded by people. She'd assumed the distinguished looking man had to be him. She'd assumed wrong.

The man stared at her. "Are you okay?"

No, she wasn't okay. Jane needed Chase Ryder. She needed…a miracle. Or the fundraising benefit she wanted to throw was never going to happen.

"Miss?"

Whatever you do, do not cause a scene. Remembering Zoe's final words made Jane force a smile. She wasn't about to risk her job or future catering jobs for the Hearth over this.

"I'm sorry," she said. "Thank you for your time."

"No, thank you." The man chuckled. "You made my day thinking I was Chase."

As the man sauntered away with a spring to his step, her shoulders slumped. She was in over her head and not qualified to do this, but she couldn't get discouraged. She couldn't give up. She still had to try.

For Emma. For sweet, four-year-old Emma who loved to play with baby dolls and still had months of treatment left, Jane wouldn't give up. Maybe she could still find Chase Ryder. It was only ten o'clock in the morning. And if not…

She would write more letters and make additional phone calls. Somehow she would find sponsors for the fundraiser. Somehow she would help Emma's mother, Michelle, tackle the mounting medical bills. Somehow Jane would pull this off.

If only she knew how.

Jane shuffled her way to the buffet table to pack up the equipment. Less than a dozen of the muffins, scones, cinnamon rolls and pastries remained on the trays, and she transferred them to a smaller plate to leave. All of the fruit cups were gone, except…

Oh, no.

One had spilled on the tile floor. Pieces of cantaloupe, grapes and pineapple had been squished, kicked and trampled on. The building's janitorial staff cleaned after events, but Jane couldn't leave a mess like this. She grabbed a towel near one of the coffee air pots, kneeled on the floor and wiped the sticky goo.

Nothing like a bit of fruit roadkill to finish off a lousy morning. She reached for a smushed strawberry. At least her day couldn't get much worse.

"Excuse me," a male voice said.

Still kneeling, Jane took in the shoes first. The black running shoes needed new laces, but looked comfortable. Just like his faded blue jeans. Her gaze traveled up the length of his calves to his thighs to his, um…

Her cheeks burned.

"You wanted to speak with me?" he asked.

What was she doing? She'd come to provide service. To beg a favor. Not stare at his… Jane jumped up. "I'm Ja…"

As she looked into his intense blue eyes, everything stopped. She couldn't breathe let alone remember her name.

From the angular planes of his face to the slight cleft in his chin to his oh-so-kissable full lips, each feature fit perfectly together with his warm, bright eyes. His blond hair fell in loose curls and brushed the back of his grayish-blue dress shirt collar and navy sports coat. No man could be so naturally good-looking. There had to be a flaw, something more than a mole or two…

And then she found it—a jagged scar running through his right eyebrow. But rather than distracting from his looks it gave him an edge, a sexy, dangerous edge. She stepped back and bumped into the table. Her heart rate increased.

"Jay?" he asked.

"Jane." Her voice sounded different, lower. She cleared her dry throat. "Jane Dawson."

"Chase Ryder."

Everything in her revolted. This was worse than before. He was too young, too handsome, too…male, like a cowboy who'd wandered into the wrong building. Wide shoulders and tall, six feet at least, as the top of her head came up only to his chin. Talk about being at a disadvantage.

"You wanted to speak with me?" he repeated.

His honey rich voice washed over her sending her temperature up at least another twenty degrees.

Don't freak out. She could do this. So what if he was the most attractive man she'd ever seen? So what if he was richer than Midas himself? A family's financial future depended on her. She couldn't be derailed by a pretty—make that gorgeous—face.

"Yes." Jane extended her arm only to realize she was holding the towel full of smashed fruit. She tossed the rag on the table and wiped her hand on her apron. "I did."

He glanced at the watch he wore on his right wrist. "I've got three minutes."

His terse response irked her, but what was she going to do? She had less than three minutes to get his help. "I'm organizing a fundraising event to assist paying for the medical expenses of a four-year-old fighting leukemia. The little girl is being raised by a single mother who works, but doesn't have health insurance."

She took a breath. "I sent two letters to your foundation about getting sponsorship for the event and left three voice mails, but never received any response. Since I was going to be here this morning, I thought I'd save another stamp and ask you myself though I realize your foundation isn't associated with Cyberworx."

He studied her, his appraising gaze missing nothing. Never had she felt so self-conscious and exposed in her freshly creased black twill pants, crisp white blouse and apron. She tucked a strand back into her ponytail.

"And you're here for…?" he asked.

"The food." She motioned to the name embroidered on

her apron. "I'm…we catered the meeting. The Hearth. It's a coffee house located in the Pearl district."

"I've heard of it," he acknowledged. "The Hearth is one of our caterers, but I don't recognize you."

"I usually work at the coffee house, not catering jobs. Except for today." Jane wet her lips. "My, um, boss said I could talk to you as long as I wasn't bothering you. Am I bothering you, Mr. Ryder?"

"It's Chase, and no, you're not bothering me."

Thank goodness. Too bad she couldn't say the same thing about him. Okay, he wasn't exactly bothering her, just leaving her hot and bothered. He might not have the personality to match his good looks, but she would still need an iced cappuccino to cool her down once she finished here. "I know you're busy and my time is almost up, but I'd be happy to send or e-mail more information about the fundraising event or buy you lunch so we could discuss it further."

He raised a brow. "Buy me lunch?"

Lunch? Had she said that? More proof she wasn't cut out for this sort of thing, but it was too late to back out now. "Lunch at the Hearth. I do get an employee discount, but we make a tasty…" Their deli sandwiches, soups and salads might not cut it for a man who could buy himself whatever he wanted. *Think. Think. Think.* "A tasty grilled panini sandwich."

The corners of his mouth lifted. "You have a lot of confidence in your cook."

A lot more than she had in herself. Zoe was going to kill her. Jane tilted her chin anyway. "It's my recipe."

His gaze met hers for a moment and a pleasurable

shiver inched down her spine. "How does one-thirty sound?" he asked.

"Today?"

He nodded once, and a curly piece of hair fell across his forehead. She ignored the temptation to push the curl back into place.

"G-great." And Jane supposed it would be. Once her heart rate returned to normal and she told Zoe that the Hearth was going to be serving grilled panini sandwiches at lunchtime today.

With seven minutes between meetings, Chase paused in front of his longtime assistant's desk. As Amanda disconnected from her call, he picked up the rake from her miniature Zen garden.

Amanda, an incredibly young looking fifty-three, gave him an indulgent smile. "Don't you have a call with Zurich?"

He checked the time. "In six and a half minutes."

"I don't want to keep you waiting." Amanda removed her headset and brushed her hand through her short, red hair. "What do you need, boss?"

He carved symmetrical rows in the sand. "Cancel everything on my schedule from one o'clock on."

She frowned. "Today?"

The same response as Jane Dawson except Amanda sounded disgusted, not surprised. He nodded.

"I should have known."

"Known what?"

"That things have been going too well for it to continue. I've managed to pick up Drew from soccer practice every night this week." She typed on her computer. No doubt, pulling up Chase's schedule. "But if there's another fire to put out—"

"No fire," he interrupted, not wanting her to worry. Amanda's job required her to be on call 24/7. He appreciated her dedication and hard work. "This is personal."

"Personal as in a dentist appointment or personal as in deciding to climb Mount Hood again?" She raised an eyebrow. "Or could it be you have a date?"

Seeing the growing interest in Amanda's hazel eyes, he scratched his right cheek. She'd worked for him for nine years and knew him better than most. She also had a tendency to mother him—the only negative trait he'd discovered. "I have an appointment."

"With a woman."

It wasn't a question. "Yes, but it's not what you think."

Amanda grinned. "How do you know what I'm thinking, boss?"

"The twinkle in your eye gives you away every time."

"I want to see the same twinkle in your eyes." Ever since remarrying after being widowed six years ago, Amanda wanted everyone to pair up. Much to the dismay of Cyberworx's single male employees. "I just want you to be happy."

"I am happy."

"You need a woman."

She sounded like his mom and sisters. He had it coming at him from all sides.

"I have plenty of women in my life." Chase had everything he wanted. He didn't need anything more. He drew a heart in the sand and crossed it out. "Just because you found 'the one' twice and remarried doesn't mean the rest of us need to follow suit." And ruin a good thing.

"Is she pretty?"

He glared at Amanda. Next time he would text message her and avoid another interrogation.

"Humor me, okay."

Chase shrugged. "I guess she's pretty."

"You guess?"

He pictured Jane. "She's got brown hair and wears purple wire-rimmed glasses. That's what I remember about her."

Not to mention her eyes. Or the way she wet her lips. But he wasn't about to mention those things to Amanda.

This wasn't a date. They were discussing a fundraiser. He liked assisting others, and Jane sounded like she needed help. Speaking of which… "Call P.J. and find out what happened to letters sent by Jane Dawson. She never received a reply to them or her telephone messages."

"Will do, boss."

"And try to find out before one o'clock."

"Sure." Amanda chuckled. "Don't forget to polish your armor before you leave."

"Very funny."

"You have a tendency to rescue damsels in distress."

"Jane's not in distress," Chase explained. "She needs help. And I—"

"Like to help people."

"Exactly." A local reporter had called Chase "the Robin Hood of the Rose City" who used a pen rather than an arrow to dole out funds to the less fortunate. Amanda had teased him about it ever since. "It's not my fault I know—"

"Everything."

"Very funny, Amanda."

"But true." She put on her headset. "One more thing before you go. What color of eyes does Jane Dawson have?"

"Um, green," he recalled. "But not what you usually think of as green, like emerald. More like peridot, my mom's birthstone."

"That's interesting." A smug smile formed on Amanda's lips. "Considering all you claimed to remember was the woman's hair color and glasses."

Busted. Amanda could see right through him. But in this case she was wrong. He only wanted to help Jane Dawson—the way he'd helped others. Her striking green eyes were simply his reward. Plus it wasn't every day someone offered to buy him lunch. Employee discount or not.

"Get back to work or I'll dock your pay." He tossed the little rake back onto the sand.

"I'm salary not hourly."

"True, but I'm still the boss."

At the Hearth, Ally Michaels poured frothed nonfat milk into the steaming drink and placed the cup on the counter for the customer.

"Nonfat vanilla latte tall." As the customer snatched the cup, Ally motioned to Kendra, the other barista, to take over the prep area and turned to Jane. "Do you know what you're going to say to him?"

"I thought I'd start with hello." Jane was in the process of trying to perfect three different panini recipes since she didn't know what Chase might like. Not the easiest task with a one-thirty deadline looming.

Thank goodness Zoe had planned on adding the hot sandwiches to the menu next month, purchased the grill and received approval from the health department, or Jane's momentary lapse of brain cells could have turned into a complete disaster. Of course, the day wasn't over yet.

Jane tasted the pesto spread. Still not right. Maybe more pine nuts.

"Hello? Not good enough." Ally pursed her glossed lips. "This isn't some random customer. It's Chase Ryder."

She said the name with an odd mixture of awe and wistfulness. Unfortunately Jane understood completely. She felt as if she was thirteen again and crushing on the newest hit boy band. Ridiculous, yes. Especially after seeing Chase Ryder's less than stellar, time-obsessed personality. But Jane hadn't been able to stop thinking about him. His eyes, his smile, his voice, his lips.

Full lips meant for slow, lingering kisses. All over.

Flutters overtook her stomach. Tingles, too.

She couldn't remember feeling this way before. Definitely not with her ex-boyfriend, Mark Jeffreys. Of course she had probably just forgotten what attraction felt like. There hadn't been room in her life for romance lately. Not with her job, classes and helping out with Emma.

And that hadn't been such a bad thing.

Except Jane liked how thinking about Chase made her feel. His aura of confidence appealed to her. Maybe she could get to know him other better and…

What was she thinking? She couldn't get lost in some daydream. This wasn't about her. Or Chase. Or what kissing him would be like. This was about Emma's fundraiser. Jane squared her shoulders. "He's just a man, Ally."

"And Mozart was just a piano player." Ally snickered. "Come on, Jane. Didn't you find Chase Ryder attractive?"

"I'm not interested in his looks, only his money."

"I still can't believe you thought he was some old guy."

"Based on your description—"

"But everyone knows what Chase Ryder looks like. He's one of the most eligible bachelors in town." Ally wiped down the counter. "Don't you read the social page in the Sunday paper?"

"I don't have time for the paper." She didn't have time for anything, not even putting on this benefit. Her hands trembled, and she flexed her fingers.

Ally studied her. "This is important to you, right?"

Jane couldn't express what the meeting meant so she nodded.

"Maybe you should put on some makeup and do something with your hair."

"Too plain?" She had grown up being called "plain Jane." Nothing had changed once she became an adult. She never had enough time or money to worry about her hair, makeup or clothing.

"You're not plain, Jane," Ally said. "You've got the girl-next-door, fresh face look down, but you need to grab Chase Ryder's attention and make him notice you."

"We're having lunch together. He can't help but notice me."

"That's not what I mean." Ally yanked a pink tube from her pant's pocket. "At least use this."

Jane caught Ally's toss. "Lip gloss? Bubble gum flavor?"

"It plumps your lips, too. You never know if he'll kiss you goodbye." Ally arched a brow. "With those lips, how could he not be a good kisser?"

"This is a business meeting, not…"

Forget it. No use arguing with man-magnet Ally. Jane concentrated on making the sandwiches instead. Too much was at stake to be distracted. She didn't want to think about Chase Ryder. She definitely didn't want to think about his lips or kissing him. Especially kissing him.

And that's when it hit her.

Garlic. The pesto spread needed more garlic.

Lots and lots of garlic.

Now she wouldn't dare be tempted by any kisses. Real or in her imagination.

Chase had never been to the Hearth. Amanda, however, swore by their mochas and pastries, which was how the coffee house had come to provide breakfast at morning meetings. He deposited coins in the meter, stuck the parking receipt on his window and walked inside.

The smell of brewing coffee, and freshly ground beans hit him first. No different from the other coffee houses in Portland, but the scent of garlic and basil lingering in the air surprised him.

And he wasn't often surprised. He'd succeeded in business by preparing for the unexpected. He didn't believe in having too much information.

On his way to the counter, Chased passed customers sitting at small wood tables. A man typed on his laptop. A woman read a book. A couple paged through the newspaper. A young man with a ponytail and wearing a familiar looking apron cleared cups and plates from one of the few empty tables. No one occupied the big, comfy looking leather chairs near the stone fireplace. The hearth, no doubt.

As a customer grabbed his drink from the counter, Chase read the menu on the chalkboard hanging on the wall behind the counter. He didn't see Jane, only an attractive young woman with long blond hair, a diamond stud in her nose and dangling beaded earrings.

"Excuse me," he said.

She—Ally according to the nametag on her apron—poured cocoa powder into a jar and didn't glance his way. "What can I get for you?"

"Jane Dawson."

Her head jerked up and cocoa spilled on the counter. "I'll be right back."

She disappeared through a pair of swinging doors. A moment later, Jane rushed out.

"Hello, Mr. Ryder, I mean, Chase." She sounded breathless. Pink tinged her cheeks. "T-thanks for coming."

She looked younger, vulnerable and he wanted to erase her apprehension. But knowing what he knew, that wasn't going to be easy. "You're welcome."

"The menu is up there." She motioned to the chalkboard he'd already read. "I'll take your order and we can sit down."

"I'd like the prosciutto and provolone panini and an iced cappuccino."

Jane's brows drew together. "Iced cappuccino?"

He nodded. "My favorite drink when it's warm outside."

"Mine, too." She pointed to an empty table. "Why don't you have a seat and I'll be right there."

He sat and checked e-mails on his PDA. This afternoon off would cost him workwise and put him behind.

Two minutes later, Jane returned with their drinks and eased into the chair across from him. She'd taken off the apron. "The sandwiches will be ready soon."

"Nice place in a popular neighborhood." He took in the surroundings. "You must do a good business."

"We do okay. Sixty percent of our business comes from

the same forty percent of customers," she said. "We stay busy all day long, but the mornings are the most hectic."

"Is that when you work?"

She nodded and toyed with her napkin.

"Contrary to what my competitors might say, I don't bite."

"Do you nibble?" The pink on her cheeks deepened and she stared into her drink.

"Only sometimes." Chase wouldn't mind one now. She was sexier than he'd realized with nice curves that had been hidden by her apron. Yes, he'd been right to come. Chase leaned back in the chair to get a better look. "So don't worry."

"Do I look worried?"

"A little."

Jane's smile lit up her face. "More like a lot, but thanks for trying to make me feel better."

He appreciated her honesty. "I'm really not that intimidating."

"Lunch is served." Ally placed the plates, each with a sandwich, potato chips and a dill pickle, on the table. "These sandwiches are a recent addition to our menu and are popular with our customers. Enjoy."

"Thanks," he said as the woman stepped away.

Jane handed him a napkin. "I hope you like garlic."

"I love garlic." He took a bite. "Delicious."

She seemed to relax and bit into her own sandwich.

"So tell me about your fundraising event," he said. "How you got involved. What you hope to achieve."

She patted her mouth with a napkin. "My father was diagnosed with leukemia five years ago."

"I'm so sorry," Chase said. "How is—?"

"He died last year."

Chase struggled for the right words. He couldn't imagine losing his dad or any member of his family. "That had, still has to be difficult for you."

Jane nodded. "During his illness, I met other families in situations similar to ours. Spiraling medical costs, little or no health insurance, the financial worries becoming as big a concern as the medical ones. I became particularly close to one family. A single mother named Michelle and her daughter Emma."

The affection in Jane's voice made the situation clearer. "They mean a lot to you."

"They are the only family I have left. We live…I live with them. I met Michelle in the hospital chapel, and we became friends. Best friends. She was concerned about her daughter. I was worried about my father.

"Emma was diagnosed with ALL, acute lymphoblastic leukemia, more than a year and a half ago. There is an almost eighty percent cure rate with proper treatment, but it's expensive. Michelle doesn't have any medical benefits with her job and she earns too much to qualify for assistance."

"So she's having to pay for this on her own," Chase said.

"Michelle can't pay for this on her own." The passion in Jane's voice matched the fire in her eyes. "She owes half a million dollars and Emma has months of treatment remaining."

This wasn't only about Emma and her mother. He wondered what scars Jane's father's illness had left on her. It was none of Chase's business, but he wanted to know.

Something in Jane Dawson sparked an interest he

wanted to explore further. Nothing more than a gut instinct, but that's why he'd accepted her lunch invitation though common sense had told him to stay away. He'd made millions by trusting his gut over common sense. "Tell me about the fundraiser."

"I want to throw a dessert benefit to raise money to help pay Emma's medical expenses."

"Why a dessert?"

"I figured it would be less complicated than a dinner."

"True, but that's a lot of money to raise in one evening."

"I know I can't raise the entire amount," she admitted. "But any amount will help them."

At least she was realistic about her goals. He respected her drive and determination. Not many people would take on such a task for a friend. "Do you have a location picked out?"

"My boss said we could hold the event here. No charge and she would donate the coffee and tea, but it might be too small."

Definitely too small.

"Which is why I'm looking for sponsors." Anticipation filled her eyes. "Would your foundation sponsor the event?"

He'd raised her hopes. Chase rubbed at his neck. He should have told her the truth as soon as he arrived, but she'd seemed so nervous. He'd wanted only to put her at ease. He shifted in his chair. "I spoke with the director of the foundation. Unfortunately we won't have the resources for another major event until January."

She blinked. Once. Twice.

Damn. He didn't want her to cry.

Her lower lip quivered. "I appreciate you taking the time to come here today."

"I wanted to come." Chase watched her pretty face and hated to see it crumple. "The foundation will make a donation."

"T-thanks."

"And I, uh, I…" All he had to do was write a check and say goodbye. That's what he should do. That's what he'd done in the past. Robin Hood, remember. Though leaving would be the smartest move, he couldn't. Not when the only thing he wanted to do was put a sparkle in Jane Dawson's eyes and a smile back on her face. "I will sponsor your benefit myself."

CHAPTER TWO

"YOU'LL sponsor the benefit?" Jane asked, afraid to hope, afraid to breath.

"I will."

What air remained in her lungs whooshed out. She uncrinkled the napkin on her lap. Talk about finding a knight in shining armor—make that denim.

No, Jane reminded herself, there was no such thing. No matter how much Chase Ryder helped, he was still just a man.

"I'll provide everything," he added. "You won't need any other sponsors."

Stuff like this only happened in dreams. Jane wanted to pinch herself. The tightness knotting her shoulders disappeared. "I don't know what to say except thank you."

"Don't thank me yet, the work hasn't even begun."

"I'm ready. You won't be disappointed." She couldn't stop smiling. Wait until she told Michelle. Maybe if the event went well, Jane could start a nonprofit group to assist other families. Wait. One step at a time. If she didn't get her hopes too high, she wouldn't be hurt. But there was one promise she could make. "I'll do whatever it takes to make this a fantastic event, Chase. I promise you that."

"Jane." The way he said her name, his voice low and

sexy, made her pulse quicken. Excitement, that's all. "I'm not just writing you a check. I want to help you organize the event."

Organize or take over? Chase Ryder didn't strike her as a follower. "You want to help? Me?"

He nodded. "We can work together."

Together? He had to be joking. The man ran a major company, no doubt he had dozens of social obligations. But the look in his eyes… "You're serious?"

He nodded.

Uh-oh. This wasn't good. Chase Ryder, philanthropist, thought he wanted to help. And he probably did until something more important came along or the workload got too heavy, and she'd be left to pick up the pieces and do it on her own. She didn't want to go through that again. Jane straightened.

"Wow," she said, making an attempt to sound enthusiastic. "That's so generous of you."

"I just want to help."

But she didn't want his help. She didn't want to rely on anyone else again.

Jane needed him to realize that working together was not a good idea without offending him. She needed him to stick to just being the sponsor of the event. "Don't you think we might drive each other crazy? It's hard to work together when you know someone, but when you don't—"

"I know I can work with you."

Yeah, because we are so much alike. She managed to keep from rolling her eyes. "We just met."

"I trust my instinct."

Ever since her relationship with Mark had ended, so did Jane. Right now her instincts shouted, "Run away, run away."

"Plus," Chase continued. "I know what I see."

"What's that?"

"Someone with a passion to make this event a complete success." He stared at her as if he could see inside her heart. "I hear it in your voice and see it in your eyes."

He had her all wrong. "That's not passion, it's panic."

"Whatever you want to call it, it's there," he said. "You know what you want to accomplish and that's where I come in. I have the contacts, the experience and the money to fulfill your vision. Teaming together makes sense."

It did. To a point.

She wanted the fundraiser to succeed, but at what cost? He might want control over all the decisions. He could change his mind and walk away. "What about the time commitment? You mentioned putting on an event like this takes a lot of work. You're so busy with your company, can you do this, too?"

"I'm the boss. I can delegate."

Delegate or shirk his responsibilities? If he could do that with his work, he might do that with the benefit.

"Besides, aren't you busy, yourself?" he asked. "You have a job and your own life to live."

"Well, yes," she said. "But the extra work is only for a short time. Once the benefit is over—"

"We can both get back to normal," he finished for her. "I understand the time commitment which is why sharing the workload makes sense."

Darn. He was right. Jane should say yes and be done with it. This wasn't about her. She had to think about Emma and Michelle, not herself.

He leaned over the table. "Don't you want my help, Jane?"

Oh, man. She was going to ruin everything if she

weren't careful. Would she ever learn…? "I—I want your help. I appreciate your offer. I really do. It's just…"

"What?"

She moistened her lips. Might as well tell him the truth. "You've caught me a little off guard."

"I'm not one for big surprises myself, but sometimes the unexpected is just what a person needs."

Chase Ryder was the last thing she needed.

But as he continued staring at her, the concern in his eyes seemed genuine. That confused her. He didn't know Michelle or Emma, yet he wanted to help. Worse, a part of Jane—a big part—wanted his help.

Why was she hesitating?

He was offering her dream come true. And, she realized, her worst nightmare at the same time. Once she agreed, she couldn't predict or control the outcome. It would be out of her hands. Just like with her father's cancer. Or Emma's. That scared Jane.

"I would like your help. I…I probably need it." What if it didn't work out? What if you're not sincere? What if…? "But have you thought this over? I mean, really considered what's involved in organizing an event? What if something came up and you couldn't help? Where would that leave…?" *Me*. "The benefit?"

He reached across the table, covered her hand with his and gave a gentle squeeze. "I won't let you down, Jane."

How many times had she heard those words or something similar before? Just once she wanted to believe that someone would follow through. That someone cared enough. That someone wouldn't leave her alone.

So all alone.

She stared at his hand, large and warm over hers. His

palm and fingers were rough, callused, as if he labored outside instead of working in an office. She didn't mind his touch. She liked it. Uh-oh. Jane tugged her hand away and grabbed her drink.

"So what do you say?" Chase asked.

What other choice did she have? She wanted the benefit to be successful. That was the only goal. She might have the "passion" to put the event together, but she couldn't do it without a sponsor. She'd be stupid if she said no. "Yes."

"Great, because I have an amazing location."

Jane held her iced cappuccino in midair. She should have known. He'd just gotten involved and he wanted to choose the venue. So much for any warm and fuzzy feelings about working together. She might as well get used to it. "Where is that?"

"My winery."

The cool glass nearly slipped from her fingers. She placed the cup on the table. Okay, maybe this wouldn't be so bad after all. "You have a winery?"

"In Stafford."

Better yet. Stafford, an upscale area south of Portland, consisted of rolling hills of green covered with estates, farms, equestrian centers, golf courses and wineries. A benefit there would draw more attention than one at the Hearth. And Chase couldn't drop his involvement if he hosted it, since his name and reputation would be on the line.

"How many guests can the winery accommodate?" she asked.

Chase raised a brow. "How many do you want it to accommodate?"

Right answer. "And we can just…use it?"

"All you have to do is pick the date."

This sounded too perfect. And that gave her pause. Nothing could be this easy. "That's all?"

He nodded. "Surprised?"

"Yes," she admitted. "I hope I don't sound rude, but what do you get out of this? Publicity for the winery?"

"No." He thought for a moment. "But that's not a bad idea. Publicity would help both of us out."

Until what he needed interfered with what she needed for the fundraiser.

"But all I really want to do is to help a little girl and her mother." An upside-down V formed above the bridge of Chase's nose. "What do you get out of all of this?"

"I get to help someone I care about," she said, feeling guilty for thinking he had ulterior motives. "Someone who's in no position to do it all on her own."

"We're not so different, Jane Dawson."

She begged to disagree, but couldn't. Not when his sincere tone told Jane he meant every word. And that meant she had not only found a sponsor, but real help.

Realization that she'd succeeded pummeled her with the force of a howling blast of icy wind from the Columbia River Gorge. She had everything she wanted. Everything plus more.

Thanks to Chase Ryder.

"What?" he asked.

"I…I'm…" Feeling inadequate, yet grateful, she shifted in her chair. Wrung her hands. Tried to remain seated so she wouldn't run over to Chase and hug him. Not that she wanted to hug him. Just thank him. "Is your name really Kris Kringle?"

"No." Chase laughed. "Though I dressed up like Santa Claus for my sister's kids last year."

"That doesn't surprise me." Jane pictured Chase wearing a white beard and red suit and being surrounded by laughing children, but then she imagined herself kissing Santa, rather Chase. That would definitely complicate matters. Blinking the image away, she resolved to remain strictly focused on the benefit. No more daydreaming and no more handholding. "So when can I see this winery of yours?"

He glanced at his watch. No doubt he had to get back to the office. "How about now?"

She gulped. "Sure."

Driving south on Interstate 5 with the pounding bass from a rock and roll song filling the Escalade's interior, Chase glanced sideways at Jane. She stared at the passing scenery—concrete, buildings and billboards—her mouth tightly closed.

So much for putting a smile back on her face and a sparkle in her eyes. He had assumed offering his assistance would do the trick, but that had only upset her more. He didn't get it. Or her. Most women watched his every move, tried to impress him or boost his ego. But not Jane.

"If you want to listen to something different—" he drove onto the I-205 off-ramp "—let me know."

"Thanks," she said. "But this music is fine."

Another mile went by. Another song played. Jane continued gazing out the window. No forced conversation trying to find common interests. No name-dropping trying to show she belonged in his world. No…anything.

Needless chatter bothered Chase, but he found her silence

both refreshing and bewildering. Other women would have talked his ears off. Why wasn't Jane doing the same?

Sure she wasn't his usual type. He dated professional women—lawyers, executives, venture capitalists—who weren't clingy and who had their money, though that hadn't kept most from wanting his, too. But Jane was still a woman. And he was a man, a rich, handsome man considered to be a "catch" if he believed his own press. Shouldn't she be flirting with him at least a little? Was she not interested in him or playing hard to get?

He would get the chance to find out.

Maybe that would compensate for the work he'd volunteered for with the fundraiser. He wanted to help the little girl, but now after the reality had set in, Chase had no idea how to make this work. He had projects to oversee, an upcoming merger and a two-foot stack of papers on his desk.

Wait until his best friend found out what he had done.

You're a sucker for a pretty face.

Sam's words had been dead-on this time, and he would never let Chase live it down.

"Nice car." Jane ran her hand along the edge of her leather seat. "It's more comfortable than my couch."

He noticed her trimmed but unpolished fingernails. Practical, like Jane herself. "That's a Cadillac for you, but you should see how it handles off-road."

"Why would you take a luxury car off-road?"

He picked up the disapproval in her voice. His normal answer "because I can" wasn't going to cut it. He would settle for the truth.

"I tried a shortcut once and ended up on forest service road then found myself on a logging road." He patted the dashboard. "It was a little hairy, but the car came through fine. I doubt I'll do it again, though."

"Smart move."

"You're right." Finally he had her attention. Good. Now he had to keep it. "That's why I bought a four-wheel drive truck. And a couple of dirt bikes."

"How many cars do you have?"

"Six," he said proudly.

"Six." She didn't sound impressed.

"Not counting the dirt bikes, a motorcycle and two race cars." He focused on the road. A white pickup pulled a horse-trailer ahead of them. "The race cars aren't street legal."

"So do you spin a wheel to see which one of the six cars you'll drive each day?"

He couldn't decide if she was being sarcastic or humorous. He would try funny. "No, I reach into a bag and pull out a key."

Her grin reached her eyes, but no sparkle. Damn, he was hoping to get both with one shot.

"You could use a dartboard," she said.

"My throwing precision would remove the element of Fate."

"Not if you closed your eyes."

There. Not quite a sparkle, but he glimpsed a twinkle in her eyes. Something stirred inside him. Something good, but unfamiliar. "Is that what you would do?"

She laughed, and the warm sound sunk into him. "If I thought I had six cars, my eyes would be closed because I would be dreaming."

The more he learned about Jane, the more he wanted to know. He exited on Stafford Road and turned right. "What do you drive?"

"I take Metro, either the bus or the MAX train depending on where I am, where I need to go and when." She touched the leather seat once again. "It's not so bad."

Not bad at all. Chase wondered what it would feel like if Jane stroked him like that with her fingertips and hand. The scene forming in his mind sent his temperature rising.

She glanced over at him. "Not as nice a ride as this, but it gets me there."

"With the scrape of brakes and the crunch of bodies."

"It's not that crowded, but…" She pursed her lips. "How did you know?"

He hadn't always driven a Cadillac. "In college, I didn't have a car so I relied on public transportation."

"Sure you did."

"I'm serious." Chase didn't want her to think he was patronizing her. "On weekends, I would take get on the Red line at Kendall Square and ride the T, similar to a MAX train, to Park Street. I'd transfer to the Green line and get off at Kenmore Square."

"Where was that?"

"Boston."

"Harvard?" she asked.

"MIT."

Her eyes widened. "MIT?"

"Massachusetts Institute of Technology."

"I know what MIT is. A top science and engineering school," she explained. "I just forgot about you being hi-tech."

"Hi-tech. Guess that's better than geek," he said. "Though it makes me sound like a robot or something."

"You mean a robotic shark that's not afraid to bite anything."

"Now that would be intimidating." He glanced her way. "Except you forgot one thing."

"What's that?"

"I don't bite. I nibble."

She looked out the window and adjusted her glasses.

Chase grinned, but said nothing, enjoying the graceful, yet nibble-worthy curve of her neck.

"What does Cyberworx do?" Jane asked.

"Lots of different things." He loved talking about his company. "Our newest division has been working with quantum dots, photonic crystals and carbon nano tubes."

Her eyes glossed over. "I'm not going to attempt a comment."

"I'm sorry."

"Don't apologize," she said. "It's not your fault I'm about as non-technical as they come. Want to know a secret?"

"Sure." Now they were getting somewhere, but he doubted she would share her favorite places to be kissed. "And I promise not to tell."

"I don't own a computer," she said.

"Not everyone owns a computer." Something wasn't adding up about this conversation, and then Chase remembered. "Didn't you offer to e-mail me information about the benefit this morning?"

"I use the computers at the library."

This complicated matters. "Do you go there every day?"

"No."

"I rely on e-mail to get things done," he explained. "It's the easiest way for me to keep in touch and contact you."

"I'll stop by the library every day and check my e-mail."

Not good enough. "I have a better idea. You can borrow one of my laptops."

"Thanks, but um…don't you need some sort of Internet access or something?"

"Yes." He recognized the flash of panic in her eyes. No car, no computer, no money. But that didn't mean she had no pride, either. He understood that. And he was beginning to understand Jane a little better. "But I have a special wireless deal. It won't cost you anything."

He waited for her reply. A beat passed. And another. She was going to say no. Somehow he would have to convince her to change her mind. For both their sakes.

"Thanks," she said instead. "That would make things easier."

He hadn't seen that one coming. She had pride, but practicality had won out. "Great."

"As long as it's no problem," Jane added.

He turned left and drove past an alpaca farm. "It's no problem."

And it wasn't. Chase got the feeling working with Jane was not going to be a problem at all especially if they could mix a little pleasure—not to mention nibbling—with business.

As Chase punched in a security code to open the double wrought-iron gates, Jane stared at the grapes growing over trellises in neatly spaced rows behind the stone wall paralleling the road. To the left sat a big building where Chase said the wine was produced. Up on the hillside, sunlight reflected off the copper roof of a grand-size house. At least she thought it must be copper. The structure looked old, built of some sort of stone or brick, like a castle or villa. She leaned forward for a better view.

The gates opened, and Chase drove inside.

Anticipation built. She felt as if she were Cinderella arriving at the castle on the night of the ball. Jane had no idea what to expect and couldn't wait to see everything. Until she remembered. Once the clock struck midnight it would be all over. She settled back against the comfortable leather seat.

A paved driveway wound up the grape covered hillside. Antique-looking lights were strategically placed along the roadside to illuminate the way at night. As they gained elevation, the house—more like a mansion—came into clear view. Jane gasped. "It's as if we've been transported from Oregon to Italy or France."

"A château in Bordeaux inspired the estate."

"The designer did his research." She truly felt as if she were part of a fairy tale. She expected to see white horses gallop by. And a prince. She glanced at Chase. "It's beautiful."

"Thanks," he said. "The first time I saw this place I had to have it. No matter what the cost."

His world was a hundred and eighty degrees from hers. She couldn't afford to rent an apartment by herself, buy a car or replace lost contact lenses. "Must be nice to be able to have whatever you want."

His gaze met hers, and her heart skipped a beat. "It doesn't suck."

Jane smiled. "If I lived here, I would never leave."

"You haven't seen the inside of the house yet."

"True," she admitted. "But I'm sure it doesn't suck."

"It doesn't." His smile crinkled the corners of his eyes. "But I don't live here."

"Why not?"

"It's too far from work," he said. "Too much traffic to deal with."

"You own a piece of paradise, and you're worried about traffic?" The question slipped out. Of course, he couldn't live here. It wouldn't be practical. She could appreciate that, especially in someone who had everything. Still it bothered her.

"I don't have patience when it comes to wasting time." He studied her. "Don't tell me you like being stuck in traffic?"

"Traffic means I can read longer." And study and do more homework. "Doesn't it seem a little sad to leave this place empty?"

"I have staff living on site." He parked the car. "I spend an occasional weekend here. And my family uses it, too."

But it didn't seem enough to Jane. She slid out the front seat and went to Chase, who had removed his sport coat and left it in the car. No need for a jacket on the sunny September day.

He pointed to a large, boxy building perched below the main house. "I want you to see the barn where we'll hold the event."

Barn? She didn't see any red paint or smell anything that suggested animals lived nearby.

As Jane followed him down a wide cobblestone path, the sun glimmered off Chase's hair. She imagined curling the ends with her fingertips. Unfamiliar warmth flowed through her veins. She needed to stop thinking about touching the man.

"Welcome to the barn," he said.

She forced her attention on the big rectangular building that resembled another château only this one was single-story. Chase pulled open one of the two sizable wooden doors.

She stepped inside. Her mouth gaped. Forget animals. No four-legged creatures would ever be allowed inside such an elegant space with hardwood floors and a vaulted, wood-beamed ceiling. "This isn't a barn."

"No, but that's what I call it."

"I'd call it perfect."

He laughed. "The winery's original owners designed the space as a reception and event site. Since wedding planners are so picky, they made sure everything was, in a word, perfect."

Chase showed where bars or drink stations could be set up. He turned on the lights to show her the kitchen with professional grade stainless steel appliances.

Back in the main room, she took in every inch of the lovely space. This was so much bigger and so much nicer than she imagined. "I can't believe anyone complained when they got married here."

"I bought the estate before any weddings took place."

"Let me guess," she said. "You made them an offer they couldn't refuse."

"Let's say I made them an offer they accepted on the spot."

"Sounds more like a gobble than a nibble or bite."

"Guilty."

Charming and kind, but still a shark. She *was* going to have to be careful around him. "I knew it."

Chase grinned. "Emma's benefit will be the first event held here."

She loved how he called it Emma's benefit. And then she realized what he'd said. "The first event here? Ever?"

He nodded. "The curiosity factory should bring people in."

The news sunk in. Okay, it actually smacked her brain and bounced off. "This is a great place for a party or dinner or a million other things. Why haven't you used it?"

"I like my privacy," he said. "My nieces and nephews run around in here when it's raining."

She tried to match the public Chase Ryder—the one who according to Ally appeared regularly in Sunday's society page—to the man standing in front of her. Tried and failed. "Thank you for allowing Emma's fundraiser to be the first event here. I'm…we're honored you'd open your home, I mean, this place to us."

"Would you like to see the rest of the estate?" he asked.

She toured the operations facility and received a glass of the winery's award winning Pinot Noir to sip while they strolled the grounds.

He showed her a dirt lot where guests could park. "We can have valets and shuttle guests up the hill to the barn."

As he pointed out where a tented waiting area could be installed, Jane tried to understand the logistics of it all. She hadn't considered parking an issue. Why should she? She no longer owned a car.

With the wineglass in hand, she followed Chase through the artfully designed gardens surrounding the mansion. Lavender scented the air. Low clipped hedges divided beds of flowers and greenery. An arbor of roses anchored one end, a fountain surrounded with colorful flowers and rosebushes the other.

"Do you know what floral arrangements you want?" he asked.

She hadn't thought that far. Not that she knew anything about flowers except the names of the most common ones. "No."

"I have two florists I use regularly, but if you have your own florist, that's fine."

A florist of her own? Jane nearly choked on her wine. The last time she'd received flowers was when her father died. "Feel free to talk to your florists."

"Are you sure?"

"Yes." Getting Chase involved would take the benefit to a higher level. That's what she needed to do to bring in the big donors. Whereas he knew exactly what needed to be done and how to do it, she knew nothing. She felt completely inadequate and totally insecure.

As he led her through the tastefully decorated *Architectural Digest*-worthy interior of the château, those feelings threatened to swamp her. By the time they reached the balcony and stared at the unobstructed view of Mount Hood, the emotions overwhelmed her. Jane couldn't enjoy the scent of flowers—bougainvilleas if she wasn't mistaken—from nearby flower pots. She fought the urge to down the remaining wine in her glass.

The estate and Chase were something out of dream, but not her dream. She knew better than to reach for the golden ring or buy a lottery ticket or wish for something that would never happen. The sinking feeling in her stomach matched the slump of her shoulders. She leaned against the railing.

"Is something wrong?" he asked.

She didn't know where to begin. Because Chase wouldn't understand. He couldn't understand.

"Jane?"

She bit her lip. Took a deep breath. Exhaled slowly. "I'm feeling a bit...a lot overwhelmed right now."

"That's normal."

Nothing about this situation was normal. She fit in at Chase's château winery as well as a barefoot, homeless orphan peddling matchsticks at Buckingham Palace. Okay, slight exaggeration. She wasn't that bad off. Jane owned shoes, lived in an apartment and had a job. But that wasn't the worst of it. She didn't have a clue what to do when it came to the benefit. That had become clear today.

What was she going to do?

She and Chase lived in completely different galaxies. Light years away from each other. How on earth could she pull this off?

CHAPTER THREE

JANE couldn't do this. She'd been kidding herself to think otherwise. If only she hadn't told Michelle about organizing a fundraiser. And approached Chase.

He took the glass from her hand. "You're trembling."

Was she? Jane crossed her arms. It didn't help.

"Come inside." He held the two glasses in one hand, pressed his other against the small of her back and led her through a pair of French doors. "Have a seat on the couch."

As she sank onto the overstuffed sofa, Chase placed the glasses on a wooden table.

This wasn't the time to be concerned about water rings, but she couldn't help reacting to his casual disregard for his beautiful furniture. "Shouldn't you put coasters down first?"

"Don't worry about it."

He grabbed a blue throw from a chair and covered her legs. She touched the soft as a feather fabric, probably cashmere.

"Would you like a cup of coffee or glass of water?"

She didn't want him waiting on her. She wanted to leave. She'd wasted too much of his time already. But she had no car, no idea where the closest bus stop might be and no cell phone to call Michelle for a ride home. Jane considered asking Chase to borrow one of his six cars until she realized that meant seeing him again to return the keys. "No, thank you."

Jane stared at the painting over the fireplace. She recognized the picture, but couldn't remember the artist or title.

He sat next to her on the couch, his thigh nearly touching hers. "Do you want to talk about it?"

"About what?" Stupid reply, but his nearness disturbed her as much as his question. One more reason to get out of here.

The upside-down V reappeared above the bridge of Chase's nose. "What's bothering you?"

How could she explain she'd gotten slapped with a harsh dose of reality while touring his estate? She'd wanted to do something she couldn't possibly manage out of love for Michelle and Emma. Jane had been swept up in a fantasy only to realize it had all been a pipe dream, not the sort of thing she could pull off. And she'd long since stopped believing in pipe dreams.

He waited and watched. For a man who had no patience with traffic, he showed an amazing amount with her. He deserved an answer, some kind of explanation.

"Would it be horrible if I changed my mind?" she asked.

"About having the benefit here?"

"About having the benefit altogether." The words tumbled from her mouth, and she felt horrible for having said them. Michelle and Emma were counting on her, but Jane was afraid.

"You can do anything you want." He stared at her, his eyes betraying nothing. "But are you sure? You seemed so excited a little while ago."

She didn't, couldn't answer. Not when a little while ago she'd been completely delusional about her abilities to organize the fundraiser.

"You feel that overwhelmed?"

His concern brought a lump to her throat. Jane nodded.

"If the thought overwhelms you so much, the work probably would, too."

"I've never behaved like this before." Regret washed over her. She expected him to be angry, not show compassion. She wanted to see his ruthless shark side. Maybe then she wouldn't feel so bad. "I'm sorry."

"Don't be sorry." His encouraging smile made her feel worse. "I've found myself overwhelmed many a time."

Chase Ryder? Overwhelmed? Maybe when he was a toddler standing on the edge of cliff alone. Jane held onto the blanket. "Are you always this understanding?"

"No, but I do have two sisters. Understanding is part of being a brother." He picked up his wineglass. "I will admit having someone to share the workload on this would have been nice."

"On what?"

"I'm putting on Emma's benefit with or without you."

Jane stared at him. "Why?"

"The medical bills still need to be paid and Emma needs more treatments, correct?"

"Yes, but—"

"She and her mother need help," he said. "It shouldn't matter who throws the benefit for them."

Guilt clogged Jane's throat. The fundraiser had been her idea. Her responsibility. Not his. "You don't have to—"

"I want to do this." He sipped his wine. "I'm thinking a black-tie event will bring in more money."

She straightened. "A bit formal for a dessert, don't you think?"

"Not just a dessert."

His eyes held a hint of mystery, a secret she wanted to know. Jane waited, until she couldn't wait any longer. "What?"

"A five-hundred-dollar-a-plate dinner with wine tasting."

Her mouth gaped. She snapped it closed.

This was no longer her responsibility. This was no longer her problem. Forget about it. That was what she should do.

But she couldn't.

"What about Emma?" Jane asked. "She wouldn't be comfortable at a formal event. Michelle, either. They want to participate, not sit at home and wait for a check to be delivered. And what about their friends who want to support the benefit, but can't afford that much."

"Isn't the goal to raise money?" Chase asked.

"Yes." That was always the bottom line for people. Jane tightened her fingers around the throw. "But there are other ways of raising money besides having people dress up like a flock of penguins and feeding them fancy foods like *foie gras*."

"You have something against *foie gras*?"

"It's the liver of force-fed geese. Fat liver is the literal translation if I remember my high school French."

He nodded once. Smiled.

The way he sat there looking gorgeous and knowing all the answers infuriated her. Turning this event into one of the fancy shindigs he normally attended was not in Emma's best interest. "I wouldn't feed that to an animal let alone pay for the opportunity to eat it."

"A lot of people would."

She wanted to wipe the smile off his face. "What about Emma? The benefit is for her. How does she fit into all this?"

"She can make an appearance at a convenient time or we can hang pictures of her on the walls."

His ideas incensed Jane. "Why not hang posters of Emma looking pale, tired and sick so people will pity her and donate more money?"

"Good idea."

"That's…that's just wrong." She stood, still clutching the blanket. "Everything you're proposing—"

"What would you do?"

She heard the challenge in his low voice, recognized the dare in his intense gaze. She thought about Emma, twirling in the living room with a purple elephant named Baby in her arms. The memory bolstered Jane's wavering confidence.

"First I wouldn't charge five hundred dollars a plate. Black-tie dress would intimidate and keep away a lot of people who might otherwise attend." *Like me.* Jane walked to the other side of the coffee table and faced Chase. "Emma needs to attend if at all possible. Think about the money we could raise if people saw her precious smile in person, heard the squeal of her laughter or saw how alive she is."

"Probably better than the posters."

"Much better." Jane rolled up the blanket. "We could put together a slide show or DVD to show people about Emma, her treatment and leukemia."

"Go on."

"Ideally, we would include children, but with Emma's low immune system we can't risk her being exposed to the germs. I like the idea of a wine tasting. Maybe we could have a commemorative bottle of wine for the event either to sell or raffle. And give each guest a wineglass etched with your winery's name to use for the tasting as well as keep as a favor. But I don't know what's involved with that."

"I can find out," Chase said.

"I see the appeal of a dinner given the space, but I believe we could accomplish more and reach a wider range of donors with a dessert buffet and silent auction with items for adults, families and children."

"We?" He raised a brow. "I didn't think you wanted to be involved anymore."

She didn't. Or hadn't. But now…

"I was simply offering input."

"I appreciate it," Chase said. "You have good ideas."

"Thanks." His compliment pleased her, more than it should. "Ideas are one thing. Implementing them is something completely different."

"I'd still like your help."

He'd opened the door, but her insecurities held her back.

"Would it hurt to try?"

If he only knew…

Could she risk it? If she failed, she wouldn't be the only one hurt. But if she succeeded, she would be able to do what she couldn't for her father.

"Otherwise," he continued, "I might make a mess of things."

Chase Ryder wasn't a man who made a mess of anything. He was smart, capable…and as manipulative as a kid bargaining for an extra hour before bedtime. She knew when she'd been had. "Like *foie gras*?"

"Among other things." He grinned, transforming himself from smooth corporate executive to mischievous charmer. "Want back in?"

"Yes." Michelle and Emma needed help, but all Jane had done was think about herself. About feeling uncomfortable. About failing. Some friend. She breathed deeply. Maybe Jane didn't know much about parking logistics or florists or a million other things, but with Chase's assistance and knowledge, she didn't need to know. "I want back in."

"Good."

"No, you're good." She tossed the blanket at him and he caught it. "You wouldn't have done any of those things you said."

"No." His deep, rich laughter curled her toes. "But you said yes."

"How did you know I would change my mind?"

"Two sisters, remember." Amusement gleamed in his eyes. "If I had a nickel for every time they changed their minds, I'd be a billionaire. Plus they taught me a few things, too."

The reverse psychology had worked on her. "Is this how you conduct business, Mr. Ryder?"

"When I have to."

"I pity your competitors." Shark or not, she knew he could be ruthless in his pursuit to get what he wanted. "They don't stand a chance against you."

A shiver of trepidation ran through her as she realized what she'd said. But Chase didn't seem aware of any innuendos in her remark. Or any doubts at all.

"You're a smart woman, Jane Dawson." Chase raised his glass to her. "You and I are going to get along fine. We'll make a fine team."

This time, she almost believed him.

* * *

Chase didn't believe it.

All these years, he'd trusted his instinct. Never had it failed him. Not until today.

As he drove Jane home, he thought about how late he'd be at the office tonight to make up for this afternoon off. And all the extra work that would pile up over the next few weeks. He'd expected to be rewarded with...well, Jane. Not today, but eventually.

Only now he knew that wasn't possible.

He'd been intrigued by Jane Dawson. No, she wasn't his type, but for all her insecurities, Chase recognized an inner strength that appealed to him on more than one level. He wished she saw it herself. He glanced at her sitting in the passenger seat. She was pretty, smart and had a heart of gold.

As much as he would have liked to pursue a flirtation or a fling, he couldn't. If they got involved, he would hurt her, as she'd clearly been hurt before. No question. And he couldn't—no, wouldn't—do that.

Jane Dawson was a sweet person, who wanted only to help her best friend. She deserved more than a guy who would treat her well, but eventually break her heart.

"Turn left at the next light," Jane said. "And get in the right lane."

Northeast Portland was filled with diverse neighborhoods—from high-priced to not-so-nice areas—that contained some of the city's finest restaurants, brew pubs and shops, but this area with congested streets and decaying, empty storefronts with For Lease signs hung on graffiti covered windows was not a familiar one. Granted, he'd seen worse areas, but he wouldn't want his sisters driving through here at night. Chase didn't like the idea of Jane walking to the bus stop or MAX station alone, but in that situation she seemed to have no fear. Or no choice.

"The apartment building is on the right," she said.

The older cinderblock structure sat back from the road with a parking area in front. He pulled into the lot and parked next to a tie-dyed painted pickup truck.

"Is the bus stop nearby?" he asked.

"Next door and across the street."

He felt better. "What about the light rail station?"

"The MAX is a block away." She studied him. "Why all the questions?"

"Curious."

And it was true. He wanted to make sure Jane was safe. The same way he would with a friend or his sisters.

The apartment complex looked clean, a mowed lawn, with only a few weeds in the flower beds and security bars on the first floor windows.

"It's a straight shot to the hospital, too," she added.

Emma. He'd forgotten about the little girl, the reason for all of this.

"I don't know what to say except thank you for everything, Chase." Gratitude laced each of her words, and made him not mind the work waiting for him back at Cyberworx. "I appreciate how you handled my embarrassing anxiety attack with such expertise. Thank your sisters for training you so well."

"I will," he said, not wanting to say goodbye. The urge to spend more time with Jane was strong though he knew nothing would happen between them. A few more minutes wouldn't hurt. He turned off the ignition.

Surprise registered in Jane's eyes. "What—"

"I'm walking you to your apartment."

She unfastened her seat belt and opened the door. "It's not necessary."

"Humor me." Chase reached for the door handle. Once she was safely inside, he could put her out of his mind and get back to work. No woman held his attention for long. "It'll be easier that way."

Her laughter brought a smile to his face. She needed to laugh more, he decided. Maybe laughing would put a sparkle in her eyes. It was probably better—smarter—if he gave up trying to do that himself.

"That's right," she said. "You're used to getting your way."

He opened the door. "What does that mean?"

"The smart thing for me to do is have you walk me to the door."

Chase followed her, noticing the subtle sway of her hips as she climbed the steps, and stood on the landing outside a door marked H.

"Would you like to meet Emma and Michelle?"

He wanted to meet the catalysts for turning his life upside down. "I would."

Jane pulled a key chain from her purse. A plastic daisy dangled from the end. "Emma can be shy around strangers, but once you're in her good graces, you're her friend for life."

"I'll remember that."

Jane unlocked the front door, opened it and stepped inside. He followed her and closed the door behind him.

A voice squealed. "Janie, you're home."

The four-year-old little girl with a short mop of curly brown hair topped by a plastic tiara bounced into Jane's open arms. "Yes, I am, jelly bean."

"I'm not jelly bean." The cute bundle dressed in pink tulle stomped her foot. "I'm a queen today."

"My mistake." Jane kissed her forehead. "I didn't notice your crown or your high heels."

Emma stared up at him. Her smile disappeared, and she plastered herself against Jane's leg. Smart kid. He wouldn't mind doing the same.

"There's someone I want you to meet." Jane's soothing tone made Emma loosen her death grip. "Emma, this is Mr. Ryder."

"Nice to meet you, Emma." Except for the paleness of her skin and the dark circles under her wide eyes, she didn't look that sick. Not that he knew what a sick child should look like. Chase kneeled. "Or should I say, your majesty?"

Emma beamed. "Oh, I like that."

He glanced at Jane, who mouthed the words "you're in." If only it was always that easy. He smiled.

"We're having spaghetti," Emma announced. "Do you want to stay for dinner?"

"That's polite of you to ask, Emma," Jane said. "But Chase…Mr. Ryder might have plans."

"Unfortunately, I do." He rose, noticing the denim slip covered couch with a stuffed lion on it, the scratched coffee table with blocks piled on top and a doll sitting on a worn, wing chair. But he saw no other clutter, not a spec of dust on the in-desperate-need-of-refinishing hardwood floors. "Maybe some other time, milady."

Emma nodded so hard her tiara fell off and hit the floor. Chase picked it up and placed the crown back on her head.

"What was that?" a female voice called from around the corner.

"My tiara, Mommy," Emma said. "But the nice man put it back on me."

Something clattered and a woman with straight blond hair rushed into the living room. "What man… Oh, Jane. You're home."

And not alone. The unspoken words hung in the air.

"Michelle Taylor," Jane said. "I want you to meet Chase Ryder. He's going to sponsor Emma's benefit and host the event at his winery."

Michelle's wide smile took years off her tired face. He extended his hand, but she hugged him instead.

"Thanks," she said. "You don't know what this means to us."

He was getting an idea. But getting hugged by a grateful stranger felt awkward when a short while ago he wanted to get romantic with her best friend. "I'm happy to help."

"Well," Jane said. "You'd better get going if you want to miss the traffic."

He glanced at his watch. Where had the time gone? "Nice to meet you, Michelle. And Queen Emma."

"Will you come back?" Emma asked.

"Jane and I are working on a special event so I'll be back." Looking down at Emma's innocent, smiling face, he felt warm all over. He glanced over at Jane, who watched them, and saw it—a sparkle in her eyes. He wanted to reach out and touch her face.

Chase looked away. He didn't belong there. He needed to get out. And fast. Before he did something he would regret.

Her Majesty Emma proclaimed the spaghetti most excellent. Dinner turned into a merry event with spilled milk, meatball races and giggles. While Queen Emma watched a video with Michelle, Jane tackled the dirty dishes.

Michelle entered the galley style kitchen. "Emma fell sound asleep. Thank goodness she already took her meds or I would have had to wake her up."

A familiar dread, something Jane had gotten used to during her father's illness, wrapped its icy fingers around her heart. It was too early for bedtime. She stopped scrubbing the skillet. "Is Emma—?"

"Just tired." Michelle dried the saucepan. "Emma had a busy day today and didn't take a long enough nap."

Tension evaporated from Jane's shoulders. "Thank goodness."

"Remember," Michelle said with a half smile. "All we can do is take it day by day."

But it wasn't easy. It hadn't been with her father. Jane didn't know how Michelle managed it with a child, trying to provide Emma with a so-called normal life without exposing her to germs, illnesses and every day injuries that happened to children. Last month, a splinter in Emma's foot caused an infection and she spent four days in the hospital.

Day by day. Repeating the mantra, Jane rinsed the skillet.

Michelle put the saucepan in the cupboard. "So tell me everything. And don't leave out a single detail."

Jane did, recounting the day for her best friend.

"The benefit will raise more money with Chase personally involved." She knew better than to get too excited, but she wanted Michelle to know help was on its way. Jane placed the skillet on the drying rack. "He knows lots of movers and shakers who can make big donations."

"All this fundraising stuff sounds great, but you're

leaving out the best parts. I want to know about Chase," Michelle said. "What's he like?"

"Chase is interesting." Jane picked up a lid from the soapy water. "He's not what I expected."

"How's that?"

"Well, he's nicer than I thought he would be. Kind and considerate. The type who would stop and help an injured dog by the side of the road."

"Really?"

Jane nodded. "I knew he was generous based on his reputation around town, but I had no idea he would be so giving. I mean, not every guy you just met would offer to fund a benefit for you and throw it at their winery."

"True." A faint light twinkled in her eyes. "What else?"

"He's an uncle and seems good with kids, at least he was with Emma."

Michelle dried the skillet. "Sounds almost perfect."

"Oh, he's not perfect." Jane scrubbed the lid. "He's a time freak who checks his watch and schedules everything down to the last minute."

"He did give up his entire afternoon to spend with you."

"True," she said. "But he buys big, beautiful houses but doesn't live in them. And he always gets what he wants. He'll play dirty, too, if he has to. And he owns six cars. More if you count the race cars and dirt bikes."

"The nerve of the man."

"I know." Jane rinsed the lid. "Who needs six cars? And more than one house?"

"Sounds like you got to know him pretty well."

"Not that well," she admitted. "Maybe I've made a few assumptions about the man."

"You think?"

"But he's sponsoring the event. That's what matters."

"He sure is a nice piece of eye candy."

"You can say that again."

"So you're interested in him?" Michelle asked.

Jane dropped the lid. Water splashed on her shirt. "Don't be silly, we have nothing in common."

"The benefit."

"We're only organizing that together, not…"

"Anything could happen."

"No," Jane said. "Because we're not…I'm not…he's not interested in me."

"He's interested in you." Michelle dried the lid. "Handsome millionaires don't go to this much trouble and offer to do this much work out of the goodness of their own hearts."

"He's just being nice." Even to Jane's own ears, that sounded weak.

"He's a man, right?"

Chase Ryder was one hundred percent male. "Um, yeah."

"Then he's not just being nice." Michelle laughed. "He's interested, too."

"He's out of my league."

"No, he's not."

Jane thought about his tendency to go after what he wanted, about how he'd maneuvered her into sticking with the fundraiser planning. If Chase decided he wanted her, she'd be in big trouble. She wouldn't stand a chance. Nor would her heart. But that was okay because he didn't regard her as a player. He couldn't. "You're wrong."

"I'm right."

Michelle had to be mistaken or tired or imagining things with that romantic heart of hers. Even after being abandoned by her lazy, rotten ex-husband after Emma got sick, her belief in romance hadn't dimmed. Better for Jane to clear up any misconceptions before things got out of hand.

"I doubt I made much of an impression compared to the type of woman he's used to dating. Even if he were interested—which he isn't—it would never work out." Jane added soap to the stockpot. "We come from different worlds. He's wealthy, educated and has traveled the world. I'm a poor dropout, trying to earn my college degree and have never even been to Canada."

"Cinderella and the prince came from different worlds, too." Michelle's wistful tone matched the faraway look in her eyes. "But they lived happily ever after."

"Happy endings only exist in fairy tales."

"You're wrong," Michelle said, her voice sad. "One of these days you're going to realize how wrong you are, Jane."

CHAPTER FOUR

SO MUCH for Chase Ryder wanting to help.

One of Cyberworx's computer guys delivered a laptop to Jane, and Chase e-mailed her with their action items and a list of caterers recommended by his foundation. But then nothing. For two weeks.

His lack of communication proved her instinct spot-on. She'd known he would let her down so she wasn't disappointed. Just frustrated. Work on the benefit stopped. She couldn't do anything. What if he disagreed with one of her decisions?

The alarm blared at four-thirty in the morning. Jane hit the snooze button. Twice. But she had to be at work by five-thirty so she shut off the alarm and slipped on her glasses.

Michelle stood in the bedroom's doorway, tying the belt on her faded yellow robe. "Are you awake?"

"I am." Jane yawned. "Just moving a little slow."

"Did you hear from Chase yet?"

Only if she counted her dreams about drinking wine and stolen kisses. Embarrassed, she crawled out of bed. "I did not."

"He's probably busy at work," Michelle said.

"I've sent him e-mails all week, but he hasn't replied." Jane knew not to count on anybody. "He's blowing me off."

"He likes you. That's why he's sponsoring the event."

Jane bit back a sigh at her best friend's totally unrealistic optimism. "Michelle—"

"Stop." She held her hand out in front of her. "No matter what you say, I'm going to cling to my fantasy about the two of you. It keeps me entertained."

"At least one of us is amused by all this."

She smiled softly. "He'll be in touch when he's ready."

"I can't wait any longer." Jane removed her shirt and pants from the closet. "I'm going to have to call him."

"Do it today," Michelle encouraged, gleefully.

"I'm not asking him out. Though I wouldn't mind telling him off."

"You can't do that."

Unfortunately Michelle was right. Jane couldn't. Like it or not, she was stuck with Chase Ryder until the benefit was over. Until then, she would have to be polite and nice and… She sighed. Was it too late to find a different sponsor?

On Wednesday, Chase sat at his desk listening to a conference call with one of the manufacturing plants. As two directors argued, he grabbed the top folder off the stack of papers on his desk. He needed to catch up on work today.

A soft knock sounded, barely audible over the heated conversation. He pressed Mute. "They can't hear us."

Amanda handed him an inch thick file. "P.J. sent this over. She said if you have any questions give her a call."

He placed the folder in his laptop case and made a mental note to thank the foundation's director.

"You've never been that involved with the foundation."

"No, but this doesn't involve the foundation directly."

"So what's going on?"

Chase wanted Amanda to attend the event, but hadn't told her anything because he didn't want her to get any ideas about Jane and him. One look at Jane's big green eyes and wide smile and his assistant would decide she'd found his match. Not that any matchmaking would succeed. He'd closed that door. Strictly business. That's how things were between them. "I'm planning a dessert fundraiser to be held at my Stafford winery."

"But you said the foundation wasn't—"

"I'm doing this on my own."

Amanda studied him. "Are you doing this alone?"

"No."

"Who's working with you?" she asked.

"Jane Dawson."

"The one you met two weeks ago?" Amanda's inquisitive gaze zeroed in on him. "The one who keeps calling?"

Damn. He forgot to call Jane back. He'd meant to, until the MFR merger hit a roadblock. "Get her on the phone?"

"Now?"

"Yes."

Amanda pointed to the speakerphone. "What about them?"

He'd forgotten the conference call. No problem. "I pay them enough to deal with it."

She inhaled sharply.

"What?" he asked.

"Nothing." Amanda smiled. "I need Jane's number."

Chase remembered he only had her home number. "Never mind I'll call her myself."

* * *

Early Friday, Jane and her crew served the rush of customers at the Hearth. The scent of baked goods mingled with the aroma of brewing coffee. Conversations drowned out the light classical music playing. The line out the door invigorated her. She loved it when the place was this busy.

"Medium cappuccino wet." She placed a cup on the service counter. "How are you this morning, Kent?"

"Tired." He grabbed his coffee. "Thanks."

"Two tall double mochas to go," Ally called out from the register.

Ignoring the bustle of the customers, Jane dosed the ground coffee into the portafilter. Holding the handle, she pressed the coffee down with a metal tamper.

"How long do you spend on each customer in the morning?"

She recognized Chase's voice, felt a hitch in her heart and nearly dropped the tamper. She didn't dare glance his way. "Thirty-five seconds if we can."

"Impressive."

"Sometimes, it is." She returned to pressing the coffee. "What brings you here?"

"My assistant loves your mochas. I'm surprising her."

"That's nice of you." With an unsteady hand, Jane inserted the portafilter in the group head of the espresso machine.

What was going on? She could do this with her eyes closed, but with Chase around she felt like a new hire on her first day during the morning rush. Ridiculous. She hadn't seen the man in over two weeks. Jane pressed the button to brew the espresso, reminding herself to pull a double shot in each cup.

"How are you this morning?" he asked.

As the espresso brewed, she poured cold milk into a stainless steel pitcher. She placed the nozzle of the stem wand one inch below the surface of the milk. She turned the knob to start the flow of steam. "That's my line."

"What do you mean?"

"Every day we ask customers how they are," she explained. "The top three answers are: busy, tired, late."

"Which are you this morning?"

As froth formed in the milk, she observed the temperature. At one hundred fifty degrees, she turned off the steam. She poured the brewed espresso into a cup, added an ounce of cocoa syrup and stirred. "Busy."

"I'd have to go with that one, too."

"I imagine so since we've been playing phone tag since Wednesday." She gently poured the frothed milk into each cup. "Did you see my e-mail last night?"

"Yes," he said. "Don't worry, we'll pick a date and caterer at our meeting tomorrow and get back on track."

Jane didn't believe him. Yes, he'd arranged a meeting at the foundation's office, but they hadn't made any progress on the benefit. "Cream?"

"Excuse me?"

She looked over at him. Big mistake. He wore a white tailored shirt with narrow blue and yellow stripes, the ever-present faded jeans and a silver-gray sports coat. The color of his jacket brought out the blue in his eyes. He seemed more handsome, taller if that were possible. "Would you like, um, whipped cream on top?"

"Please." His easy smile stole her breath. "On both."

Ignoring the rapid thud of her heart, she topped the mochas with whipped cream, fastened on the rounded plastic lids and placed the two cups on the counter. "Two tall double mochas."

"Thanks, Jane." He took the cups. "Do you need a ride to the meeting tomorrow?"

"Short cappuccino dry," Ally called out.

"No, thanks." The less time Jane spent with Chase, the better. She preferred dealing with the faceless, concise, impersonal Chase Ryder via e-mail or voice mail. Much simpler than dealing with the attractive, intriguing, perceptive man in person. She grabbed a small cup. "I have a ride."

He raised one of the mochas in a half wave. "I'll see you tomorrow, then."

He sauntered past the line of customers. She wanted him to stop and look back.

"Earth to Jane."

She glanced at Ally. "What?"

"Short cappuccino dry."

"Sorry." Jane stared at the door. No sight of him. Her shoulders sagged.

Ally laughed. "You've got it bad."

Not yet. But Jane would soon if she wasn't careful. Chase Ryder was a dangerous man. She just hadn't realized how dangerous until now.

Waiting in the lobby of his foundation's office building on Saturday morning, Chase checked his watch again. Jane should have been here seven minutes ago.

He rose from a chair and walked to the receptionist's empty desk. No one worked on weekends here. That was why he'd selected the location. Plus the office had planning resources and was close to public transportation.

He wanted to get this meeting over with and be on his way. No, he really wanted not to be here at all.

Chase stared out the window at the rain pounding against the asphalt. The dark, overcast day matched his mood.

Stopping by the Hearth had been a mistake. Up until then, he'd e-mailed Jane about the fundraiser, left her messages on her machine and managed to ignore her existence otherwise. Okay, maybe a random thought here and there, but pursuing anything more with her was a complication he didn't want nor need in his life. She was simply someone he was working with not a beautiful, desirable woman.

But that's who he'd found making his coffee yesterday.

He'd never expected her to be so alluring behind the espresso machine. Her flushed cheeks and wide smile had instantly improved his morning and made him wish it were the weekend. He'd wanted to steal her away from her normal life, not to mention his, and do something wild, crazy...sexy.

Stupid.

Chase shook his head, trying to erase the image forming in his mind. The physical attraction he understood, but that didn't explain his irrational behavior. And that was how he'd acted these past twenty-six hours and—he glanced at the time—nineteen minutes. Irrational.

He had used her name when he changed his password. Worse, he'd mentioned her to Piper, his older sister, setting off an onslaught of questions through the evening from her, his mother, and finally his younger sister, Hannah, who called from New York. Thanks to them, Jane was always on his mind now.

And that had to stop.

Before he did something else stupid like asking her out

or kissing her. Jane didn't seem the type to indulge in a casual fling. He had too much going on for anything else. They were not a good combination. Chase looked at his watch.

Where could she be?

She didn't have a cell phone, so he dialed her home number. The line picked up.

"Hello," Jane's voice said and that irritated Chase. She shouldn't be at home. "You've reach Michelle, Emma and Jane. Leave us a message and we'll call you back."

Damn. A message.

She must be on her way. Or lost. Unless she couldn't get a ride. Or forgot.

No, Jane wasn't the type to forget. Not when they'd spoken about the meeting yesterday. The urge to pace was strong, but before he could stand, the door to the office opened. A hooded figured walked in, rain covering the purple raincoat.

An unfamiliar relief hit Chase. He didn't like the feeling. "About time."

"Sorry I'm late." Water dripped from her rain slicker onto the floor. She set down several plastic shopping bags. "I'm making a mess."

"It's just water."

She pushed back her hood. Wet tendrils of dark hair plastered against her face. "I had to wait for the MAX train."

"You said you had a ride."

"I did." She wiped the rain from her face. "But Emma woke with a fever. Michelle had to take her in."

"I would have picked you up."

"It's only water." Jane shrugged out of her oversize coat, uncovering a backpack underneath. She wore a black long-sleeved T-shirt and a pair of well-fitting jeans that showed off her curves and round bottom. "I like walking in the rain."

He liked how she looked after walking in the rain—all wet with her hair tousled. Seductive. He wondered if this was how she looked when she showered. No, he reprimanded, do not go there.

"I used to walk in the rain with…"

"Who?"

"My dad." She cleaned off her glasses. "Do I smell coffee?"

Chase nodded, wishing she hadn't changed the subject. He wanted to know more about her father and her. "Just remember I'm not a professional barista."

"As long as it's hot and strong—" she removed her backpack, and her shirt stretched over her breasts "—I won't be disappointed."

Desire slammed into him like a slap shot at the buzzer.

Jane smiled. "Ready to get started?"

Oh, yeah. Chase swallowed.

What the hell was he doing?

He had to look beyond the attraction. Concentrate. Focus. He pointed to the doorway. "We can use the conference room."

"Great." She picked up her backpack and he helped her carry the plastic bags. "While we talk, we can do a taste test of the desserts the three caterers provided."

Chase didn't care who they picked, but she wouldn't decide herself. At least he could enjoy the samples. He led her inside. His laptop was open and his files stacked.

She pulled out a spiral notebook, a manila envelope and her laptop. "Looks like you've been here a while."

"Not that long."

Jane set out the desserts in three groups. As she opened the containers the mouthwatering aroma of chocolate filled the air. "Are you always on time or early?"

She made punctuality sound like a fault. He grimaced, but decided if they had a few conflicts, maybe he wouldn't feel such a strong pull toward her. Chase sat down on the other side of the table from her. "Are you always late?"

"Usually." She reached for a bite-size brownie from group one. "Which means we'll have to cut each other some slack."

He was going to have to do a lot more than that.

Chase surveyed all the desserts. The sensual expression on her face tempted him to try a brownie, too. Tasty. She could be a serious distraction to what they needed to accomplish. "So what's on the agenda besides tasting desserts?"

"We need an event date." She flipped the page in her notebook. "Michelle gave me a couple of dates based on Emma's treatment schedule. The second weekend in November is her first choice. That would give us six weeks."

"Plenty of time." As Chase pulled out his PDA, he found himself mesmerized by Jane eating a chocolate covered strawberry from group two. She parted her lips and slowly took a bite. Talk about sweet torture. He had to look away.

He checked his calendar. His parents' anniversary was that Saturday. His family would like Jane. Too much, probably. It would be easier to go alone. "What about Friday night?"

"Friday night works for my friends, but what about yours?" She placed a miniature éclair from group three on a paper plate and handed it to him. "They're the ones with the big pockets."

"I'll convince them to open their wallets no matter what night we have the event."

She wrote in her notebook. "Friday is our date then."

Jane bit into her own éclair. A drop of custard filling remained on her lips. The pink tip of her tongue darted out and licked it off. His temperature shot up twenty degrees.

Needing a distraction, not to mention a cold shower, he typed the date into his PDA. Maybe tasting desserts wasn't such a good idea.

"You understand Emma might not be able to attend," Jane said. "With her low immunity system anything can happen. Michelle hates making plans because they never work out. She feels like she's tempting faith or jinxing it somehow."

"That doesn't sound like a fun way to live."

"It's not." Jane's voice quieted. "You live with the threat, the fear of…relapse."

"Isn't Emma in remission?" he asked.

"Yes, but so was my father at one time. Unfortunately nothing is a certainty."

Sadness flickered in her eyes. But before he could say anything, do anything, she asked, "Don't you like your éclair?"

Business, he reminded himself. Strictly business.

"It's fine." She looked unconvinced. He took another bite. "It's great. So what's next on the list?"

"Food." She removed papers from the manila envelope. Covered with scuffmarks and scribbling, the envelope looked as if it had traveled around the world. Twice. "What do you think of the desserts so far?"

"I like the group on the right so far. Number one."

"Me, too." She grinned. "Those brownies are to die for."

So was Jane's smile. "Who's the caterer?"

"Trevor Cabot," Jane said. "He's got a great reputation, and he's cheaper than the other two."

"Isn't he usually the most expensive?" Chase asked, remembering an article he'd read about the up and coming caterer.

"Initially he was, but I explained what the benefit was for and he offered a discount." She took a mini cream puff. "I showed him a picture of Emma from my wallet and he dropped the price more."

"Talk about being resourceful." Chase laughed. "Are you sure you haven't done this before?"

"Nope."

She dipped her fingertip into the whip cream and licked it off. Lucky finger.

"I bet you could teach me a thing or two."

She blushed. "Maybe."

"Definitely." He stared at her, wanting to discover everything she was thinking and feeling. And that bothered him. He shouldn't care about those things. Not when they concerned Jane Dawson.

"Okay, we've picked our caterer. I can cross that off the list." She marked on a piece of paper. "Now we have to settle on some sort of theme for the evening."

He appreciated her keeping them on track. Left to him they'd probably end up…in trouble. He tugged at the collar of his suddenly too tight T-shirt. "Any ideas?"

"Yes, but I'm not wild about any of them." She adjusted her glasses. "But we need a theme so we can pick the invitations and plan the decorations."

All of this was going to take time. Not just today, but over the next six weeks. Being with Jane wasn't smart. He was going to make a mistake. Better to stop now.

He tapped his pen on the table. "I have an idea."

She leaned forward. "What?"

It took every bit of self-control not to stare at her breasts straining against the fabric of her shirt. The door he'd closed was slightly ajar and wanting to be wide-open. Remember, strictly business. "The foundation uses a party planner for its events. Let's bring her on board to help us."

Jane straightened in her chair. "Why?"

"She's a professional," he explained. "She'll know what kind of theme will fit an event like ours. She'll arrange for everything we need, at a discount."

"Whatever the discount, I'm sure it won't cover her fee."

Jane seemed so worried about the finances. Most people wanted him to spend his money, usually on things far less worthy than a fundraiser event. "So? We're hiring a caterer."

"Because we can't make the food." She met his gaze. "But we can select a theme, choose invitations, figure out the decorations. And the more we save on the expenses, the more money we clear for Emma and Michelle."

A valid point. Beauty and brains were a potent combination. One he found difficult to ignore. His susceptibility to her only increased his reluctance to give up on the party planner idea without a fight. "It will save us time and work. I'm willing to finance it."

"But it's unnecessary." Jane's nostrils flared. "I'll be the first to admit I'm on a steep learning curve here, but I'm figuring it out. And we've only started brainstorming the theme. It's not like we've exhausted every idea."

She sounded defensive and a little upset. That wasn't his intention. "I'm not questioning your abilities, Jane. I'm positive we could come up with a great theme."

"Then let's do it." Relief filled her eyes. "There's no reason to hire a party planner."

"You weren't so certain when we started all this. Wouldn't you like a little help with the planning?"

"I thought I had help." She pursed her lips. "You."

Another point for Jane. But this was more for her sake, not his. He didn't want to hurt her. "It would be easier on you—"

"Don't use me as your excuse, Chase."

"It's not an excuse." But after he said the words, he realized it was. What choice did he have? Something about Jane pushed his self-control to the limit.

"If we hire a party planner, we're dumping the whole event in her lap. She might have great ideas for the black-tie crowd and put on dozens of parties every month, but Michelle and Emma might feel uncomfortable and out of place." Jane set her jaw. "Michelle trusts me to do this, and I want the night to be special, to be perfect for them. That means I have to do it."

He respected her loyalty to her best friend. "Jane—"

"Don't worry." Her mouth tightened. "You won't need to do anything else, Chase."

"What did you say?"

"I'm letting you off the hook." She crammed the manila envelope, a folder and papers into her pack, zipped it up and stood. "You're obviously too busy to help."

"You can't fire me."

"No, I can't." She rose and slung her backpack over her right shoulder. "But this shouldn't be such a burden on you. I'll update you on my progress via e-mail. It's not a problem."

"It's a problem to me," he said. "Sit."

She remained standing.

Damn. Chase liked seeing her show some spunk. The lack of confidence she'd experienced at the estate no longer seemed to weigh her down. He knew she had an inner strength, but he didn't like the way she stared at him as if he were a traitor. "Working on the fundraiser is not a burden."

"If you remember when I approached you, all I asked for was financial sponsorship for the benefit, not organizing assistance." She arched a brow. "You usually leave these things to your charity foundation, right?"

"That's the way it's been in the past."

Her eyes darkened. "Go back to writing checks, Chase. I'll do the rest."

"Jane, we don't need to hire a party planner." His plan had not only backfired, but exploded in his face. "You're right. We want this to be the right party for Emma. We should handle these details ourselves. It was a bad idea. I'm sorry."

She didn't look convinced, but she sat.

"I want to do this, Jane."

"I have to know you're serious about this, Chase." Her voice sounded strained. "I can't worry you'll disappear on me in the middle of this."

"That's not going to happen." He would work on his self-control, keep his distance and not look at her. Easy enough. Yeah, right. "I've said it before, but I won't let you down. Emma and Michelle, either. I promise you."

"But what if you do?"

A beat passed. He raised his chin. "Name your price."

CHAPTER FIVE

JANE couldn't believe how much they'd accomplished during the meeting—decisions made, layouts drawn and a schedule agreed upon. Chase hadn't let her down after all. She smiled. "That about covers everything except the theme."

"We can brainstorm this week." He glanced at his watch. "Do you want to grab lunch somewhere?"

Her hungry stomach nearly answered for her, but she had two dollars and forty-one cents in her wallet. Not enough money for lunch out with Chase. And she didn't want him to pay for her. That would be too much like a date. He'd gone casual and cute today, a navy T-shirt worn under a white dress shirt with the tails hanging out and dark jeans, and she'd avoided looking at him during the meeting by keeping her eyes glued on her papers, the desserts and her laptop. But at a restaurant, she'd have no choice but to gaze into his dreamy eyes. No, she didn't want to even contemplate the word d-a-t-e. "I, uh, can't."

"May I drive you home?"

If he'd really wanted to go out with her, he would have tried to convince her, right? But he hadn't. She bit her lip.

"It's raining hard." He packed his laptop. "And I bought Emma a present. I'd like to give it to her."

"That's sweet." His thoughtfulness touched her. "Emma loves presents."

He helped Jane on with her raincoat before putting on his, an olive-green coat with no hood. No wonder his curly hair looked a bit wild and unruly. And sexy. Now all she had to do was survive the drive home with him.

At the apartment, she called out for Michelle and Emma. No answer. Jane checked the answering machine, but no messages. They must still be at the hospital, but if it were serious, Michelle would have called. "Do you want to wait for Emma?"

"If you don't mind."

"It's no problem." Jane wouldn't be rude to the man who held the purse strings to the fundraiser. She'd pushed her luck enough this morning, but his wanting to hire a party planner aggravated her to no end. She'd taken his suggestion personally, assuming he didn't have faith in her abilities, which were valid given her meltdown at the winery, but she'd come far since then. Though Jane's doubts over Chase's commitment to the event remained.

He removed his raincoat. She hung their wet jackets on the coat tree. "If you're hungry, I can fix lunch."

"I don't want to intrude."

He already had. "I don't know about you, but after all those desserts I'm hungry for real food."

"I thought you didn't want lunch."

"I wanted to be home in case Michelle needed me," she said. "Want something to eat?"

"Okay. That would be great. Thanks."

She took a step toward the kitchen and stopped. "Lunch won't be fancy. Soup and sandwiches is all I have."

"That's fine."

She handed the television remote to Chase. "You can watch TV until lunch is ready."

He placed the remote on the coffee table, next to a shoebox filled with makers and crayons. "I'd rather help you."

"Uh, okay." Michelle shared cooking duties with Jane, but she couldn't remember a man, well except her father, offering to help in the kitchen. "That would be, um, great."

Chase followed her. "What can I do?"

She grabbed a can of tomato bisque soup from the cupboard. "Want to be in charge of the soup?"

"I can do that."

"Thanks." She placed the can, the can opener and a saucepan on the counter. "Here you go. Pour the soup into the pan and—"

"I know how to heat up a can of soup."

"Oh, sorry," she said, her cheeks warm. "A lot of men—"

"Can't cook?"

She nodded. "My father tried his best and…" Mark, her ex-boyfriend, never had offered to wash the dishes. "Well, not every guy cooks."

"I do." Amusement gleamed in his eyes. "Not every day, but I'm comfortable in the kitchen or in front of a barbecue grill."

"You should have no problem with the soup."

He opened the can. "No problem at all."

She removed bread from the cupboard. "Do you want turkey and cheese, peanut butter and jelly or grilled cheese?"

"Turkey and cheese."

"That's what I'm having, too," she said.

"Great minds think alike."

The common phrase didn't mean anything, but no one had ever said she had a great mind except her dad. And he was biased. Or so she thought. She felt good about her work on the benefit and about herself, and pleased Chase seemed to agree.

As he poured the can of soup into the pan, a warm feeling settled over Jane.

He glanced her way. "What?"

Embarrassment rushed through. Her insides burned. No doubt, her cheeks matched. She couldn't believe he caught her staring at him. "Do you want mustard or mayonnaise?"

Chase set the empty can on the counter. "Both please."

As she made the sandwiches on the cutting board, she was aware of Chase's every movement. From the way he seasoned the soup with extra salt to the way he stirred. She felt comfortable making lunch with him, and that disturbed her more than she liked.

A door closed. Michelle and Emma.

"I'll open another can of soup," Chase said.

"Wait a minute." Jane walked into the living room. Michelle sat on the couch cradling a pale Emma. Every one of Jane's muscles tensed. "Hey, jelly bean. How are you?"

"I don't like fevers." Emma pouted. "They gave me an IV."

Jane caressed Emma's soft hair. It was growing back curlier than before. "I'm sorry, sweetie."

Emma sighed. "Everyone's sorry."

"Hello there," Chase said, his voice quiet.

Michelle's eyes widened. "Hi."

He kneeled next to Emma. "Are you hungry?"

"I want my mommy." She buried her face against Michelle, who rocked and kissed her.

Chase backed away. "You can have whatever you want, Emma."

Jane felt useless. Nothing she offered to do would help. When Emma felt bad, only Mommy would do. And poor Michelle. She looked as if she were on the brink of collapse.

Emma sneaked a peek at Chase, but said nothing.

"I have a present for you." He retrieved a white bag from near the front door. "This is for you, your majesty. Open it when you're ready."

Emma clutched the bag's handles.

"Thank you, Chase. That's so nice of you," Michelle said. "I think we'll rest for a few minutes first."

"We're making lunch if you change your mind," Jane said.

As Michelle plodded down the hallway holding Emma, tears stung Jane's eyes. She hated seeing them like this. Emma's illness took such a toll on mother and daughter. It wasn't fair.

Chase placed his hand on Jane's shoulder. "You okay?"

With him by her side… No, that wasn't possible. "I will be. Thanks."

"And Emma?"

"If it was serious they would have kept her at the hospital."

"So it's good she's home."

"Yes." His gentle touch comforted her, but Jane longed for Chase to hold her, to feel his warmth and be surrounded by his strength. She looked up at him, not knowing whether to move closer or back away. His gaze held hers as if locked together by some invisible means. She couldn't break the contact if she tried. "One time when Emma's fever spiked, Michelle called the doctor and they sent her straight to the hospital where they had a room waiting for her. So having Emma home is good."

He raised his hand from Jane's shoulder to cup her face. Leaning on him for support would be so easy. That's what she wanted, what she needed. She struggled against the temptation.

"It's okay," he said.

She rested her cheek against his callused palm. Just for a second. That's all she needed. But it felt so good. He was so strong. Solid. How long had it been since she'd allowed herself to lean on anyone? Too long.

"Jane."

His voice sent a shiver of anticipation racing down her spine. He was going to kiss her. Her heart rate kicked up three speeds. She wanted him to kiss her. Jane parted her lips.

Soft.

His gentleness surprised her. His lips moved over hers as if she were the most cherished woman in the world. And that's how Jane felt. She didn't want the feeling to end.

His kiss caressed, erased the hurt and sadness. Nothing bad could happen; nothing could go wrong as long as she was with Chase. And she wanted to be with him like this. More than she thought possible.

His kiss teased and explored and lingered. She was defenseless against him, but she didn't care. Not as long as his kisses continued.

They did.

She drifted into paradise. She never knew a kiss could

be so…precious. She waited for him, expected him to draw the kiss to an end, but he didn't.

And Jane couldn't be happier.

Sensation pulsated through her. She desired more, so much more. He moved his hand, brushing his fingers through her hair. She leaned into the kiss, into him. Solid and strong. Chase's heart beat against her chest.

Not a shark, but a man.

A gorgeous, generous, gracious man.

The pressure against her lips increased, and a soft moan escaped from her. He jerked away.

"The soup." Chase dropped his hand from the back of her head. "I forgot about the soup."

The soup? She remembered. Lunch.

As she followed him, disappointment mixed with relief. Jane had wanted him to keep kissing her, but that wouldn't have been smart. She knew that logically, yet that's what she'd wanted. More than she'd wanted anything in a long time.

Chase raised the pan off the stove and stirred the bubbling liquid. "So much for impressing you with my cooking abilities."

But he'd impressed her with his kissing abilities. She picked up a knife and sliced the sandwiches in half. "We got distracted."

"Yes, we did. At least the soup didn't burn." He placed the pot back on the stove. "Though it needs to cool down."

No kidding.

Jane needed to cool down and cool it. She had to think about Emma, the benefit, her heart.

Someone like him would only end up hurting her. And even though she had wanted to kiss him—wanted him to kiss her again—she didn't want to be hurt. "Chase about what—"

"I hope you don't mind," Michelle's voice interrupted them. "Emma decided she wanted to have lunch instead of a nap."

The little girl cuddled a pink princess cloth doll. No doubt the present from Chase.

He opened a cupboard and grabbed another can of soup. "We'd love to have lunch with her majesty."

"Yes, we would." Jane's talk with Chase could wait. It wasn't as if he was going to kiss her again. "One peanut butter and jelly sandwich coming up."

Chase strapped on his climbing harness as he stood next to the health club's rock wall. He'd considered canceling his usual Sunday afternoon exercise with Sam, but Chase needed to take his mind off Jane and what had happened yesterday.

It had just been a kiss.

Not a big deal, but he wondered if Jane agreed. Questions had glimmered in her eyes. Questions that lingered unspoken over lunch. He hadn't been prepared to answer them. Any discussion would have been awkward. Chase wasn't sure how he felt, let alone what to say about having kissed in Jane's living room. He'd been relieved when Michelle and Emma joined them.

Sam pulled off his sweatpants to reveal a pair of climbing shorts. A woman passing them stared boldly at his best friend's tall, champion swimmer physique, but as usual, Sam didn't even glance back. "So what's she like?"

"What's who like?" Chase asked.

"Jane," Sam stuck his baseball cap in his bag and rubbed at his short brown hair. "That's her name, right?"

Not him, too. Chase reached into his chalk bag, pulled out the ball and rolled it around his hands.

"Come on." Sam prepared to belay him. "Tell me something. Anything. Piper isn't going to let this one go."

Chase didn't need this. He shoved the ball back into the bag. "Tell Piper to mind her own business."

"She's curious."

"Try nosy."

Sam nodded. "You know your sister."

"She's your wife." Chase attached the clip to the rope. "Can't you make her submit or something?"

"You have no idea how marriage works."

He reached for a hold. "And I don't intend to find out."

As Chase climbed, Sam pulled the rope and cinched it in place. The two made a good team. They always had.

He and Sam Baylor had been the dynamic duo, flirting and partying as they left a trail of broken hearts from downtown Portland to Mount Hood. That was until Piper, Chase's older sister, returned from a job in London. One look and Sam fell. Chase gained a brother-in-law, but lost his partner in crime.

"Seeing you led around on a leash by my sister is enough to convince me I want no part of marriage. Ever."

"You don't know what you're missing out on, pal," Sam said.

"I'll take my chances."

"So this Jane. Is she sexy?"

Chase missed a hold and fell a couple feet. The rope caught him. He regained his footing and glared. "Shut up, okay."

Sam saluted him then pulled on the rope.

Chase climbed to the top and rappelled to the ground. Sweat beaded on his face and dripped down his back.

"Either your skills are going soft—" Sam laughed "—or you're distracted today."

Chase wiped his face with a towel. "No thanks to you."

"I saved your neck up there," he said. "You owe me. So tell me what's the deal with you and Jane?"

"We're working on the fundraiser." Except being with her felt more like play even when they disagreed over something like the party planner. And he couldn't forget how Jane, with her sweet nature and caring personality, was so easy to be around.

"Just spill, dude."

"Why is that so hard for everyone to believe?" he asked.

"Because you're not…"

"What?"

"You're not that generous, Chase."

Tossing the towel into a basket, he grimaced. "What are you talking about? Between the foundation and my own donations I give away—"

"I'm not talking about money, Chase. Everyone knows your willingness to give your fortune away." Sam brushed his hands together and wiped them on his shorts. "But you've never been that generous with your time."

Chase hadn't. "But that doesn't mean—"

"Why else would you be doing it?" Sam's gaze pinned Chase. "Tell me why and I'll drop it."

He tried not to think about Jane's green eyes, her soft smile or her hot curves. He silenced the sound of her warm laugh and the passion in her voice. "The goodness of my own heart."

"Try again, buddy." Sam laughed. "What does she look like? Pretty?"

"Off the record?" As Sam nodded, Chase took a swig from his water bottle and considered Jane. "She's pretty, but it's not her looks. There's something about her. I haven't figured out what yet."

"That's more thought than you've given anything since the MFR merger talks started," Sam said. "Body?"

"Slim." She had curves. He'd seen them when she wasn't hiding them under aprons or clothing. He'd felt them pressed against him. His groin twinged. Chemistry, that's all.

Not true. He enjoyed being with her in the meeting, making lunch, listening to her messages on voice mail. But that didn't mean…anything.

"So what's the problem?" Sam asked.

"She's not my usual type."

He laughed. "That could be a good thing."

"That would be a very bad thing." Chase remembered standing in Jane's living room and seeing the vulnerability in her eyes. Making her feel better had been his only goal. He hadn't considered the risks or the consequences. He'd simply acted. He did that a lot around Jane, when he was more guarded and cautious with other people. "The women in my life know the score. They don't put demands on me. I don't put demands on them. The arrangement works for all parties involved."

"It works for you." Sam raised a brow. "I doubt it works for anyone else."

Chase shrugged. "I don't hear any complaints."

"But Jane would complain."

"She's the picket fence type."

"Looking for Mr. Right?"

"I don't know, but that's what she needs," he said. "Someone to take care of her."

"But not you."

"Not me."

Chase wasn't looking for a commitment. Once he had almost considered settling down, but luckily didn't. He had everything he could want. He didn't need anything else.

"But she's pretty and slim." Sam rubbed chalk on his hands. "Nice?"

"Very."

"Fix her up with one of your friends," he suggested.

"I could." Chase ran through the list of his single buddies. Rick, Jace, Brody, Matt. He pictured one of them holding her in his arms and kissing her. Not going to happen. "But I wouldn't want her to get hurt."

"So you care about Jane."

It wasn't a question. Chase prepared to belay Sam. "You've been spending too much time with my sister."

"Doesn't mean I'm not right."

"I don't know Jane that well," Chase said truthfully, which made all these feelings about her so…weird. "And that's how I intend to keep it."

No matter how tempted he might be to kiss her again, it wouldn't be good for Jane. And Chase had a funny little feeling it wouldn't be good for him, either.

Monday afternoon, Jane stood outside Chase's office. She held his folder in her hand. Somehow it had gotten mixed up with her paperwork, and he'd e-mailed saying he needed it back. She considered mailing it, but he hadn't mentioned anything else in his e-mail. Nothing about the fundraiser, nothing about the kiss they'd shared. That convinced her to bring the folder by in person. She wanted—no, needed—to fix this.

"He'll be right with you, Jane." With stylish red hair and a suit the color of an espresso, Amanda Newberry seemed more like a CEO than an assistant sitting at her desk. "Would you like something to drink?"

"No, thanks." Jane felt like she should be the one getting the coffee and emptying the trash. She stared at the shaded glass walls of Chase's office. She'd known how nice the Cyberworx meeting facility was, but she hadn't expected a guy who wore only jeans to have such an elegant office. She straightened the collar on her white blouse and wished she wasn't in her coffee house clothes. "Beautiful building."

"Yes, it is." Amanda smiled. "How is the planning going?

"Good." Or at least it had been until Saturday. Jane couldn't forget how seeing the tenderness and concern in Chase's eyes had affected her, but she had to put that behind her. "We still need a theme."

"You'll find something you both like."

As Jane nodded, the door to his office opened. Chase stepped out. No blue jeans today. Her mouth went dry. He wore a well-cut, dark gray suit with a blue dress shirt and an even bluer striped tie.

The prince and the pauper. That's how she felt compared to him. She clutched the folder, bending the edges.

"Hello, Jane." His charming smile assaulted her, sending her tummy into backflips. He seemed totally unaffected by her appearance. Not that she expected a welcome kiss or hug. "How is Emma doing?"

"Better." The word took a tremendous effort to say. His assuredness and confidence intimidated her. If she were smart, she'd leave before she lost herself in his expressive eyes.

"Sorry you had to wait," he said. "I was on a video conference call."

"It's okay." She handed him his folder. "Here you go."

"Thanks, but I could have picked it up."

"It's no problem." Or hadn't been until he'd walked out looking more gorgeous than a *GQ* cover model. Maybe a discussion about the kiss wasn't the best idea right now. "I'd better go."

"Come inside first."

She should beg off. Seeing Chase like this left her unsettled and anxious. "I—"

"Just for a minute," he said. "Please."

With reluctance slowing her every step, Jane walked past him and into his office. Modern. Sleek. Expensive. The interior matched the man himself. "Nice digs."

"Yes, they are." His gaze raked over her, making her feel like a mouse inside the lion's den. "Feel free to look around."

"Thanks." She wanted the opportunity to gather herself. "I will."

A U-shaped desk took a third of the office. His PDA sat in a portal next to his laptop that was connected to a desktop of some sort. Stacks of paper covered one side. Two pictures set on the other side. One of children—his nieces and nephews?—and the other a family portrait. She picked Chase out right away. He looked younger, and he didn't have the scar over his right eye.

The phone rang, but he ignored it.

Framed covers of magazines and articles about him and Cyberworx hung on the walls. "I didn't realize you had so much press coverage."

"It's not me." He snagged a blue squishy ball from his desk and tossed it in the air. "It's Cyberworx."

She read one of the plaques. "Two thousand and one Entrepreneur of the Year. Impressive."

And more than a little intimidating.

"My mom thought so," he said.

"She must be proud of you." The words slipped out.

"You know mothers."

But Jane didn't. Her own had died when she was a baby. There had been only her and her dad. And now there was only her.

The phone rang again.

She knew he was busy, but she wondered what his day must be like. All the paperwork, meetings and phone calls. No wonder he didn't have a lot of free time.

A hockey stick rested against a display case containing manuals, magazines and several glass items. "You play hockey?"

"Used to."

There was so much she didn't know about him, but everything she discovered pointed out how wide the gulf was between them. "The few times I ice skated, my ankles bent in."

"It takes practice to strengthen your ankles."

And she hadn't had the time or money to practice. Some things never changed.

The phone rang once more, but again he didn't answer.

Jane walked to a round table with four chairs in front of a nice big window.

"Jane—"

"About what happened on Saturday…" she said at the same time.

"You go first," Chase said.

"I was upset about Emma. Sad."

"I know." He placed the squishy ball back on his desk. "I wanted to comfort you."

"You did." But he'd also made her feel important and cared about.

"I hope so." He scratched his chin. "But I, uh, forgot myself. Stepped over the line. I'm sorry."

"Don't be." She hadn't expected an apology; she hadn't wanted one. The idea he regretted the kiss stung worse than a yellow jacket wasp. "It was nothing."

His gaze met hers, but he remained silent. Obviously he agreed with her or he would have spoken up.

"I mean we're just working together." She swallowed around the latte-size lump in her throat. Chase's kiss had not felt like nothing to her, but she wanted—needed—to downplay his effect on her. Her heart might be on the line here, but so were her pride and her ability to work with this man so Michelle and Emma could have a future. "It won't happen again."

"We are." His eyes never left hers. "And it won't."

Jane's body—her lips, in particular—rebelled against the words. "We don't need any complications."

"No, we don't need any of those."

His words were a hallow victory. She'd never felt so safe, so secure before, as she did that day with Chase. But that wasn't worth the risk of more kisses. She couldn't afford to believe in the illusion. Jane forced a smile. "Good."

"Yes, good," he said. "Strictly business will be our motto. Now all we have to do is come up with a proper theme."

Great, she thought, back to the benefit, but she felt a twinge of disappointment he'd dropped the subject so easily. When would she learn? "Any ideas?"

"How about a Robin Hood theme?" Chase suggested. "Sherwood Forest. Merry men in tights. Maid Marian."

"Steal from the rich to give to the poor?" She tilted her chin. "I don't think so."

"Hey," he said. "I'm just trying to lighten the mood."

"Forgive me for not laughing." How could she have ever kissed the man? So what if he was handsome? He was also irritating and frustrating. Worse, she was stuck working with him. "Strictly business doesn't mean monkey business, Chase."

A vein on his neck throbbed. "Trust me, Jane, I won't make that mistake again."

CHAPTER SIX

IT'S NOTHING.

All week, Jane's comment about his kiss annoyed Chase. She'd wanted the kiss; she'd enjoyed the kiss. He wanted to prove how wrong she'd been to say it was nothing.

Except he couldn't.

Not when he agreed with her wisdom of no more kisses.

Keeping things strictly business, though, hadn't improved their productivity. All progress had screeched to a halt thanks to disagreements over the theme selection. And that forced them to schedule another face-to-face meeting. He wasn't looking forward to it.

Saturday morning, Chase parked a half block away and walked to the foundation's office. Jane stood in front of the building. She wore an old oversize red field coat, a pair of tan corduroy pants and brown clogs. With her hair in a ponytail, she looked more ready for a morning stroll through an orchard than a meeting. He liked the comfy, country style on her. Not that her clothes mattered to him.

He unlocked the door. "You're early."

"I had to open the Hearth." She held two coffees and a brown paper bag. "At least we have nourishment to get us through this."

Jane waltzed past him and into the conference room. She removed her coat and placed it on a chair.

Chase noticed the appliquéd butterflies on the front of her brown T-shirt. Staring was probably not the most prudent action. He pulled out his laptop. "I thought you worked this morning."

She placed pastries and slices of coffee cake on a paper plate. "I did."

"Where's your uniform?"

"In my backpack. I wear it enough during the week so I brought a change of clothes." She handed him a coffee. "One tall double mocha with crème."

"Thanks." Ever since meeting her, Chase had wanted to help her. But with the exception of the benefit, he'd been the one on the receiving end in this relationship. Working relationship, he clarified. "But you didn't have to go to so much trouble."

"No trouble." She sat at the table. "I needed to eat."

Tension crackled between them. Was it the arguments over the theme or something more? "Well, I appreciate it."

She sipped her coffee. "So the theme…"

Straight to business. Relieved, he grabbed a pastry. "Why don't you like A Starry, Starry Night?"

"I love the painting, and if this were a fundraiser for an artist or studio or museum, it would be a great theme." She took a slice of coffee cake. "But this is for Emma. Vincent Van Gogh cut off his ear. Not appropriate for a four-year-old girl."

"And you think A Night To Remember is appropriate?"

"Yes." Jane clenched her jaw. "It will be a night to remember with wine, chocolate and the silent auction."

"All we need is for donors to associate the benefit with

the book and movie about the *Titanic*." He smirked. "I do see the resemblance to a sinking ship, though."

As she sipped her coffee, her hand trembled.

Every part of him went on alert. "Are you okay, Jane?"

"It's been a…long week."

"Is it Emma?"

"No, she's doing great." Jane picked at her piece of blueberry coffee cake. "It's school. Silly really."

"It's not silly if it upsets you." He leaned back in his chair. "What's going on?"

"I dropped out of college when my father got sick," she said. "But he wanted me to graduate so I've been squeezing in classes when I can."

Chase had no idea she was also a student. "That must be difficult working full-time."

She nodded. "I ran into a snag this week. I need to take a prerequisite class, but it conflicts with my work schedule. I'm going to have to wait until it's offered again." She pushed the coffee cake away. "And that will delay…everything."

"I'm sorry," he said. "Can you adjust your hours?"

"Yes, but if I switch shifts I lose my manager's pay." She ran her fingertip along the edge of her coffee cup. "I can't afford to do that right now."

Chase could write her a check to cover her salary. He wouldn't miss it. "Jane, I want to help—"

"Thanks, but no. I'm sorry I mentioned it. We should get back to the event." She wiped her hands with a napkin. "But at least you know why I've been a little more…combative."

The word amused him. "Is that what you call it?"

She shrugged. "What would you call it?"

Foreplay. No, that wasn't right. "Passionate."

"You think?"

"We are both passionate about…our theme ideas."

His gaze caught hers, and she looked at her notebook. "Maybe we should throw out our ideas and start over."

"Sure." Maybe they could start over, too. No. That wouldn't change anything. "We've got nothing to lose."

"I'll kick us off, or rather Emma will." Jane removed a piece of paper from her notebook and slid it across the table to him. "Emma had her own theme suggestion."

"It can't be worse than anything we brainstormed." He studied the paper covered with pink and purple crayon scribbles. "What is this?"

"Princesses." Jane sighed. "Emma wants us to throw a princess party complete with her favorites Cinderella and Snow White. She thought everyone could dress up and we could give tiara's and magic wands for the favors."

"Cute, if we were inviting the under eight crowd. My nieces would love it," Chase said. "But it might be a hard sell to everyone else."

"That's why I was hoping we would agree on something else first." Jane spun her pen like a baton. "Emma said you told her she should get whatever she wants and she wants the event theme to be princesses."

"I didn't think she heard me."

"She did, and plans on holding you to it." Jane blew out a puff of air. "That means we have a princess problem."

"I don't want to disappoint Emma."

"Me, either." Jane dropped the pen. "She's been through so much already. But we can't—"

"I know." But this was also Emma's fundraiser. He wanted to include her. "We'll have to incorporate her princesses into whatever theme we choose."

Jane's eyes widened. "You're kidding."

"I'm not."

"Do you know how hard that's going to be?"

"Yes, but…" Chase remembered a book he'd read to his nieces. "Her favorite princesses are from fairy tales, right?"

Jane nodded. "Disney movies, some based on fairy tales."

"Let's use a fairy tale theme."

She was quiet. Too quiet.

"Do you have a problem with that?"

"It's just—" Jane bit her lip "—could we please skip anything having to do with happily ever after?"

"What's wrong with it? My parents have been married for thirty-seven years."

"Good for them," she said, not meeting his eyes. "Not everyone is so lucky."

"Don't you believe in happily ever after?" he asked.

"I… This isn't about what I believe or not."

But she didn't believe. Whoever broke her heart had done a hell of a job and deserved to be punched in the jaw.

"What's your concern?"

"Emma is in remission, but anything could happen." Jane's strained tone matched the sadness on her face. "Living happily ever after is the goal, but we don't want to jinx it."

He considered her words, considered what would be appropriate for Emma and Michelle. "I agree, we shouldn't use happily ever after as our theme."

"Thank you." Relief filled Jane's eyes. "We'll think of—"

"Once upon a time," he interrupted.

"Once upon a time?"

"For our theme," he said. "The architecture gives the winery an old world feel. All we need to find are some fairy tale inspired decorations and centerpieces."

"I don't believe it, but it works for me." She wrote in her notebook. "And Emma will love it."

"But what do we do about her princesses?" He took a sip of coffee. "They aren't exactly my strong suit."

"Come on, you've never dated a princess?"

Humor laced each of Jane's words, but Chase didn't think she'd find his answer funny. He had dated a princess. Two actually, but one's country no longer existed.

He scratched his neck. Wished the fault line running up the West Coast would pick this exact moment to shift. Wondered what the odds of Mount Hood erupting in the next ten seconds might be.

"So you have dated a princess," Jane stated.

"How—"

"The sheepish look in your eyes gave you away."

"It's not sheepish," he said. "It's…concern."

"Concern over what?"

"Your, um…"

Chase rose from the table and turned on the coffeepot. He should have answered her original question. That would have been easier.

She drew her brows together. "My what?"

He sat. "Your, uh, feelings."

"Oh." She smiled at him as if he were a child being praised. "But who you date doesn't bother me. It's not like we're, um, you know—"

"I know." Which made him feel like an idiot for bringing it up. One kiss didn't mean she would swoon at his feet. Yet the way she'd responded when he kissed her,

An Important Message from the Publisher

Dear Reader,

If you'd enjoy reading contemporary African-American love stories filled with drama and passion, then let us send you two free Kimani Romance™ novels. These books will keep it real with true-to-life African-American characters that turn up the heat and sizzle with passion.

By the way, you'll also get two surprise gifts with your two free books! Please enjoy the free books and gifts with our compliments...

Linda Gill

Publisher, Kimani Press

Peel off Seal and Place Inside...

We'd like to send you two free books to introduce you to our brand-new line – Kimani Romance™! These novels feature strong, sexy women, and African-American heroes that are charming, loving and true. Our authors fill each page with exceptional dialogue, exciting plot twists, and enough sizzling romance to keep you riveted until the very end!

KIMANI ROMANCE ... LOVE'S ULTIMATE DESTINATION

Your two books have a combined cover price of $11.98 in the U.S. and $13.98 in Canada, but are yours **FREE!** We even send you two wonderful surprise gifts. You can't lose

Two NEW Kimani Romance™ Novels

Two exciting surprise gifts

YES! I have placed my Editor's "thank you" Free Gifts seal in the space provided at right. Please send me 2 FREE books, and my 2 FREE Mystery Gifts. I understand that I am under no obligation to purchase anything further, as explained on the back of this card.

PLACE FREE GIFTS SEAL HERE

DETACH AND MAIL CARD TODAY!

168 XDL EF2L

368 XDL EF2W

FIRST NAME

LAST NAME

ADDRESS

APT.#

CITY

STATE/PROV.

ZIP/POSTAL CODE

Thank You!

(KR-TL-11/06)

If offer card is missing write to: The Reader Service, 3010 Walden Ave., P.O. Box 1867, Buffalo, NY 14240-1867

BUSINESS REPLY MAIL

FIRST-CLASS MAIL   PERMIT NO. 717-003   BUFFALO, NY

POSTAGE WILL BE PAID BY ADDRESSEE

THE READER SERVICE
3010 WALDEN AVE
PO BOX 1867
BUFFALO NY 14240-9952

NO POSTAGE
NECESSARY
IF MAILED
IN THE
UNITED STATES

pressing her mouth against his, it hadn't been casual. Chase would put money on it. "I thought—"

"I mean," she continued on over him. "It's not like it would bother you if I'd gone out with say, a prince."

"Have you?" Damn. He hadn't meant to ask that question, but now he wanted to know the answer.

"No princes."

Absurd relief washed over him. Of course she hadn't dated a prince. Jane wouldn't give a prince the time of day. But that didn't mean there hadn't been other men, ordinary men who might have swept her off her feet. "What about a guy who acted like a prince?"

"Nope."

Not that he cared. He didn't. Care. That was. But he wanted to punch the guys she'd dated for not treating her better. The ones who got to kiss her without worrying about crossing some line. Though there may not have been as many of those during her father's illness. "Do you go out—?"

"Shouldn't we be discussing the benefit and not my personal life?"

"Right. Strictly business." Chase said the word for his benefit, not hers. "Sorry. I got…distracted."

Jane typed something into her laptop. Her eyes focused on the monitor.

"What?" he asked.

"Give me a minute."

Chase gave her two. When he rose and tried to see what she was doing, she shielded her monitor from him. "No peeking."

"Didn't you learn how to share in kindergarten?"

"No, we learned how to stand in line and keep our hands

to ourselves," she said. "Sharing wasn't taught until first grade, but we moved a lot that year so I never got that lesson."

Chase sat, watched and waited.

A minute and a half later, a smile lit Jane's face. "I found it."

He leaned forward. "What?"

"A way to incorporate the princesses without using their actual images." She turned her laptop so he could see the screen filled with pictures of supplies for a fairy tale wedding. "We could use symbols to represent each of Emma's favorites."

He pointed to a glass slipper, a castle and a carriage. "Cinderella."

Jane nodded. "Wouldn't the castle or the carriage be great centerpieces? We could auction them off, too."

Always resourceful and practical, that was his Jane. "You are amazing."

Gratitude shone in her eyes. "Thanks."

"What do we do about Snow White?" he asked.

"I was thinking—"

"A dangerous thing, I'm discovering."

She grinned. "Emma received a free trip to visit Disneyland from a charity organization. She loved the statues of Snow White and the seven dwarfs near a wishing well. So I was thinking we could have a wishing well and ask guests to fill out cards with messages for Emma and place them inside for her."

"Another great idea." He hoped Jane could see how talented she was at this. "Have you ever thought about being an event planner? You're a natural at this."

She stared at her laptop's screen.

"I'm serious."

Jane glanced up at him. "Thanks."

She looked so adorable Chase seriously regretted sticking strictly to business. But he'd only hurt her if he started something, and he was damn sure not going to be the one who took that last bit of sparkle from those eyes. "So where can we find the stuff we need?"

"On the Internet—" she pursed her lips "—or a party store that sells wedding supplies."

"Let's go," he said.

Standing with Chase amid the white and pastel filled aisles at the party store made Jane wish they had ordered the items over the Internet. She would rather be anywhere— including the dentist's office strapped in the chair for a root canal—than here in the middle of wedding planning central. But Chase had cut a deal with the store manager for a discount and free delivery of the items they purchased so they weren't going anywhere.

"Look at all this stuff." A mixture of horror and awe filled his voice. In his faded jeans, gray T-shirt and a navy pullover he looked out of place among the overflowing shelves of tulle, lace and flowers. "No wonder people hire wedding consultants."

"It's a lot to take in, but you'll get used to it."

"I'll never get used to a place like this." His deer-in-the-headlights shock gave way to man-in-the-sanitary-napkin-aisle befuddlement. "I don't think I would want to."

"Let's get what we came for and go." As she guided the cart down the aisle, one wheel wobbled and another clanked against the tile floor. "We wouldn't want any wedding mojo to wear off on us."

Chase's brow furrowed. "I thought women liked weddings."

"I like weddings as long as they're not my wedding."

"Finally a woman who understands."

If he only knew. She nodded.

On the last aisle past the tiaras, place cards and favor bags, they found the gold carriage centerpieces. Each came with ivory-gold-trimmed ribbon and a small pillar candle. Jane wrote the item number on the purchase order. "So we need fifteen."

"Thirty," Chase said.

"That's too many for one hundred and fifty guests."

"P.J., from my foundation, said to plan for at least two hundred and fifty."

Jane ran the numbers through her head. More tables, favors and food. The food. "But the caterer is planning—"

"I spoke with him," Chase interrupted. "The increase isn't a problem. But he needs a final headcount the week before."

She stiffened, annoyed. "When were you going to tell me?"

"I thought I had." Chase examined a crystal Cinderella slipper. "It doesn't matter, does it? We should be happy for the increase in numbers."

His nonchalant attitude irritated her more. "I'd be more happy if you would have told me what was going on."

"I'm sorry," he said. "I will keep you in the loop. We're in this together, Jane."

Unfortunately she wasn't so sure. She pressed her lips together.

Chase held a sand castle centerpiece. "What do you think of this?"

Two hours later, they finished filling out the purchase order and headed for the checkout register. They walked around a gaudy display for bachelor and bachelorette parties. Chase stopped and fingered a purple feather boa. He picked it up and draped it around Jane's shoulders. "You look great."

She blew the feathers away from her face. "It takes more than a fancy boa to make plain Jane look great."

"You're not plain, Jane." That upside-down V formed above his nose. He added a red boa. "Far from it."

Using the boas, he pulled her toward him. The feathers tickled her neck. Closer. The intensity in his eyes sent a surge of heat running through her veins. Even closer. The sight of his parted lips reminded her of their last kiss and her heart pounded in her ears. Closer still.

Heaven help her, Jane wanted him to kiss her. She knew better, but standing this close to him she didn't care. He lowered his mouth to hers. Instinct kicked in. Self-preservation at all cost. "We said no more kisses."

"I changed my mind."

"But it might complicate things."

"I don't care." His hot breath fanned her face. "Do you?"

Did she? Her pulse raced. She opened her mouth, but didn't—couldn't—answer.

Chase didn't give her a second chance. He covered her lips with his and kissed her. Hard.

Heat exploded and shot throughout her body.

He kissed her as if he couldn't get enough of her. With urgency, need, hunger. He left no part of her mouth untouched.

His first kiss had made her feel cherished. This kiss made her feel desirable, sexy, alive.

She clutched his shoulders and held on. Afraid to let go because he might stop.

She didn't want him to stop, not ever.

"Clean up on aisle seven."

The voice bellowed through the store. Chase stopped kissing her and released the ends of the boa.

Her cheeks flush, her insides on fire, Jane took a step back. Then another. She couldn't believe he'd kissed her in the store. Or that she'd kissed him back the way she had.

Jane struggled to control her ragged breathing. "What happened to strictly business?"

The tilt of his head made him look almost…shy. "Would you like an apology?"

"Do you feel the need to give me one?"

He raised his chin and met her eyes directly. "I'm not sorry I kissed you again."

"Then don't apologize."

"I won't." The corners of his mouth curved. "But I might need another kiss."

Chase Ryder went after what he wanted. He wanted…her. A shiver inched down her spine.

"Yes. No." She inhaled sharply. "I mean…"

"What do you mean, Jane?" His gaze raked over her as if she were tomorrow's stock market report. "What do you want?"

You.

Oh, no. It was true. She wanted him. Her lips still tingled from his kiss and her body retained the warmth of being pressed against his.

He brushed a hair from her face. "What are you thinking?"

That no matter what he said or how wonderful his

kisses, a plain Jane like her couldn't hope to hold her own against a Prince Charming like him. She knew better than to believe in fairy tales. She would only end up yearning, hurt and alone.

"We shouldn't let this keep happening." She struggled to remain calm. "Why does this keep happening?"

"I wish I knew."

"Maybe." She hesitated, unsure and battling conflicting emotions. "Maybe we should try to be friends."

"Friends?"

"Yes, friends." But the word sounded empty and the idea foolish. Too late. Jane removed the boas. She went to place them back on the rack, but Chase stopped her.

He took them from her and placed them in the shopping cart.

She glanced at the basket, then at him. "What—"

"Not a word, my friend," he said. "Not one word."

One word described Chase's actions today—*stupid*. Kissing Jane in the middle of the party store proved only a fine line separated genius from the insane. He needed to have his head examined. That was certain.

Jane wanted to take the MAX train home after they finished shopping. He let her go. What else could he do when the tension buzzing between them reminded him of the high-energy beams of a particle accelerator? If they stayed together, they would no doubt collide. Explode.

Chase grabbed the shopping bag from the passenger seat of his Escalade. He glimpsed red and purple feathers, tossed the bag into the back of the car and walked into his house.

Plain Jane.

She'd tried to be funny when she called herself that, but he'd glimpsed the vulnerability in her eyes and her belief in the nickname. He'd wanted to show her how wrong she was. He'd wanted to kiss her. And she wanted to be friends.

Friends.

He assumed she didn't mean friends with benefits. No, she meant friends who exchange Christmas cards and e-mail each other on their birthdays. Chase sat on the couch and turned on the television. A college football game filled the big screen.

He wanted more than that and he couldn't keep lying to himself that he didn't. He wanted to kiss her. Again. Forget friendship. He'd never experienced such a rush of longing for a friend. Or any woman for that matter.

Friends.

How could Chase be her friend when his feelings constantly betrayed him, chipping away his resolve? He found Jane Dawson irresistible. Her looks, her mind, everything.

Why does this keep happening? She'd asked the question. He wanted to know the answer, too. The visiting team scored a touchdown, but the kicker choked and missed the extra point.

Maybe Jane wasn't the reason, but his circumstances were. Maybe he'd been working too hard. Maybe he needed a date.

A date with a woman who didn't set his skin on fire and cloud his mind. Someone who wanted to have fun and nothing else. Someone who wasn't Jane.

Chase couldn't continue on this path. He had to do something to stop obsessing about her, her soulful green eyes, her generous mouth, the lilt of her voice.

The only question was—what?

CHAPTER SEVEN

Sunday night, Jane stood at the entrance to aisle four and smiled. Volunteering at the Keller Auditorium would take her mind off Chase. She could forget about their kiss and the lack of an e-mail or a phone call from him and enjoy being back at the theater. She missed the anticipation of the crowd as curtain time drew near, the excitement as the music played and the escape watching a show could provide. Attending the theater had been one of her most favorite hobbies until her father got sick.

"Hey, Jane, long time no see," an usher in the lobby said. His bald head gleamed from the lights. "Where have you been?"

"Hi, Fred." She adjusted the stack of programs in her hands. "I haven't had time to volunteer lately. Too busy with my job and school, but Dotty Brees was sick tonight, so they asked if I could fill in."

"Well, it's good to see you," he said. "I'd better get to my post or there will be trouble."

In the lobby, patrons sipped drinks and purchased souvenirs.

"How long is intermission tonight?" a man in a polo shirt and khakis asked her. Behind him stood a well-coiffed woman in a tight black dress and a restless looking teenage boy with more body piercings than Jane could count.

"Intermission is only fifteen minutes long so we recommend preordering beverages."

He took two of the programs she offered.

"An usher can help you locate your seats." Jane handed the boy a program, but he gave it back. "Enjoy the show."

Or at least try not to hate it too much. He didn't look the type to appreciate the romantic comedy—the kind of musical Jane used to love. She liked nothing better than seeing a show, tapping her foot to the beat and laughing. She hadn't had much time for that lately, but maybe that would change.

As she distributed more programs, Jane heard laughter. A beautiful woman, in a shimmering blue cocktail dress, flipped her luxurious mane of chestnut hair behind her shoulder and placed her hand on...

Chase.

His shoulder, actually.

But it didn't matter where.

Jane's heart pounded in her throat. Her stomach knotted. She clutched the programs to her chest.

And tried not to care.

So what if he'd kissed her yesterday? So what if he was out on a date with someone else tonight? Jane was the one who had suggested they be friends. She shouldn't care who he was with or what he did.

But she did. A lot.

Her heart felt as if it had been cut in two. Ridiculous.

Two kisses did not make a relationship, no matter how incredible they had made her feel.

"Can we have a program please?"

"I'm so sorry." She focused on the two gentlemen, one in jeans and a T-shirt and the other in a dark suit, and handed them each a program. She repeated her standard speech, barely aware of what she was saying and directed them to the usher.

The men thanked her.

She glanced over at Chase, but he was gone. His date, too. Relief mingled with anxiety. She wasn't sure which was worst—knowing where he might be or wondering when he might show up.

Jane concentrated on passing out programs, but Chase remained on her mind. Maybe she wouldn't see him again. Maybe she'd imagined seeing him. Maybe—

"Jane?"

No. She focused on the programs in her hand. Please don't let it be him. But she could recognize his voice anywhere including the crowded and noisy lobby at Keller Auditorium.

"Welcome." As their gazes met, a shock ran through her. Jane hated how attractive he looked in his black suit and white shirt. Still she had a job to do and pasted on her best at-your-service smile, something she had perfected during her father's illness. "Would you like a program?"

He glanced at the nametag/ID worn around her neck, surprise on his face. "You work here, too?"

"I volunteer," she explained. "Anyone you see in white and black is a volunteer. The ushers, who are paid, wear navy."

"I had no idea you—"

"Who's your friend, Chase?" The knockout in the designer dress stepped forward bringing with her a waft of exotic smelling perfume.

His sharp intake of air was the only clue he wasn't comfortable with the situation. Or maybe the woman's perfume was a little too strong for him.

"Shannon Landry," he said, his voice cool and collected as always. "I'd like you to meet Jane Dawson."

"A pleasure, Jane." Shannon placed her fingers possessively around Chase's forearm. She might as well stick a Don't Touch, He's Mine tag on his suit lapel. "Do you work at Cyberworx?"

"No," Jane said.

Shannon's confused, but interested glance passed between Jane and Chase. "So how do you know each other?"

"We're organizing a charity event," he said.

His cool, detached tone irked Jane.

"Oh." Shannon's tight smile relaxed. "With the foundation."

"No, just us," Jane added.

Shannon stared down her nose. "How…interesting."

"Isn't it?" A blonde with a dark-haired man stepped forward.

"Hello, Jane," the blonde, in a red dress, said warmly. "I'm Piper Baylor, Chase's sister, and this is my husband, Sam."

Sam—tall, dark and handsome—shook her hand. "Hi, Jane."

She recognized the couple from the family portrait on Chase's desk. "Nice to meet you."

"It's a pleasure to meet you," Piper said. "How is the dessert coming along?"

Jane noticed Piper had blue eyes like Chase. "Okay."

"I love the theme."

"You can thank your brother for that," Jane said.

Chase took a step. "Let's sit down."

Piper frowned. "But—"

"Not now," Sam and Chase said at the same time.

Shannon looked irritated and puzzled, but beamed when Chase placed his hand at the small of her back to get her moving. "Thanks for the program, June."

"It's Jane," she corrected, though she figured the slip had been intentional. "Enjoy the show."

As the four of them walked toward the front of the orchestra section, Piper glanced back, but Chase didn't.

"Welcome." Jane handed programs to an elderly couple and recited her spiel. The way they held hands brought a tear to her eye. She blinked.

"Thank you, dear," the gray-haired woman said.

Jane gave programs to the patrons rushing in at the last minute, but she remained aware of Chase, where he sat, what he did. Not once did he look back at her.

And that hurt.

It was as if he hadn't seen her minutes ago, hadn't kissed her yesterday. She felt…invisible as if she were a stranger passing our programs, making coffee, living next door. That's how she'd felt for years, but it hadn't mattered. Not until meeting Chase.

The lights dimmed, and with them Jane's fake smile. As the orchestra played from the pit, the music swelled to a crescendo. She slumped against the wall.

Jane had known her entire life that she never belonged at the ball. That the glass slipper would never fit. The enchantment she had felt with Chase could only last until midnight. And the clock had struck twelve a long time ago.

So why did it hurt? Why did seeing Chase with another woman hurt so bad?

* * *

Chase stood on the sidewalk outside Keller Auditorium as the crowds passed by. People raved about tonight's show, but he'd barely heard a word of the performance. He couldn't recall one song. All he could think about were his mistakes.

Asking Shannon out had been his first. Chase had realized that the minute he met her in front of the fountain across the street from the theater. She was beautiful and smart, a high-powered advertising executive, but discussing parties, vacations and work no longer interested him. He'd wanted a distraction, but being with Shannon had only reminded him of why he would rather be with Jane.

Joining Piper and Sam for the musical had been Chase's second mistake. After meeting Jane, Piper had become her champion. She had pulled him aside during the intermission to tell him not to blow his chance with Jane. Not the makings of a pleasant evening. Nor the next family gathering.

And his third mistake… Chase wanted the opportunity to fix that one.

He watched the auditorium's employee entrance. Thanks to a twenty-dollar bill he'd given an usher, Chase knew where the volunteers exited. Several musicians, carrying instrument cases, left the theater. The flow of people dwindled.

A short, stocky, bald guy opened the door, and Jane walked out. She saw Chase and stopped. "What are you doing here?"

Feeling foolish and out of his element, he straightened. "You shouldn't walk alone at night."

With her lips pressed together, she stared at him. She wasn't smiling and the spark had disappeared from her eyes once again. His fault? Chase didn't want to know the answer.

The old guy grunted. "Want me to take care of him, Jane?"

"No thanks, Fred," she said. "He's okay."

Fred, who had to be at least sixty, eyed Chase warily. "You sure about that."

"Yes," she said.

"Well, I hope we see you around here more."

"Me, too."

Fred slunk away, glancing back at least twice.

Chase rocked back on his heels. "You have a protector."

"Fred knew my dad." Jane shoved her hands in her coat pocket. "Where's Shannon?"

That didn't take long. "We drove separately."

Chase didn't know what else to say. Indecision gnawed at him. He was used to making million dollar decisions and taking action. So why couldn't he do the same with Jane?

"Do you want a ride?" he asked finally.

"I don't mind taking the MAX."

"I mind." He motioned the way. "I'm parked down the street at a garage. I'll drive you home."

She bit her lip. He expected her to say no.

"Okay," she said.

A surprise, but a pleasant one. "Let's go then."

Jane fell in step beside him, walking on the street side of the sidewalk. He shifted to the other side of her.

She gave him a curious glance. "Why did you do that?"

"It's safer if you walk on the inside of the sidewalk in case a car drives up on the curb."

"I can take care of myself."

"I know, but it's a habit of mine."

A car honked. A bus drove by. A siren wailed. The sounds of the city did nothing except amplify the silence between them.

The light turned and the Do Not Walk sign flashed. He waited next to her at the crosswalk.

"I'm sorry about tonight," he said. "I hope I didn't make you uncomfortable."

"Uncomfortable isn't the word I would use."

She wasn't making this easy on him. Of all the days for her to show her backbone. He would have smiled if he could. "I didn't know you would be there."

"Would that have changed your plans?"

"I…I don't know." The confusion in her clouded eyes matched his own. "I feel as if I did something wrong and hurt you. I didn't want that to happen. Shannon isn't my girlfriend. We've gone out before, but that's all."

"You don't owe me any explanations, Chase."

The light changed. Jane stepped off the curb and crossed the street. He lengthened his strides to keep up with her.

"Don't run away, Jane."

"If I was running away, I wouldn't be here now." Her gaze locked with his. "What do you want?"

You. He did, but for how long? "I wanted to apologize."

"You've done that." Her pace increased. "You can drive me home and forget about it. And me."

He touched her shoulder. "Wait."

She stopped, but looked at the pavement.

Chase raised her chin with his fingertips. "I don't want to forget about you. About what we—"

"There is no we." She turned her head so he was no longer touching her. "Strictly business. Friends. Remember?"

He wanted to forget those words. "You can't deny the chemistry between us."

"Chemistry doesn't change how I feel when I'm around you."

"How is that?"

"Out of my league."

He hadn't expected that. "Why?"

She gazed up at him through half-lowered lashes. "Because of who I am, Jane Dawson, barista, and who you are, Chase Ryder, Mr. Cyberworx."

"We're not so different," he said.

She pursed her lips. "So you've said before."

"I'm serious, Jane," he explained. "My parents didn't have a lot of money. They couldn't afford to send me to MIT so I had to do it myself with a job, loans and a scholarship.

"I started Cyberworx in a rental house in a not-so-nice area of Portland. Six of us, including my brother-in-law Sam, lived there because we couldn't afford rent anywhere else. Sometimes it was a choice between a piece of equipment or food. The food lost out."

"But now…"

"It's different. I'll be the first to admit that. I enjoy where I am now, but I haven't forgotten where I started." He cupped her face. "I know what you're going through. And I respect what you're doing. Your job, classes, the benefit. You're an amazing woman, Jane. Smart, funny, sexy. So very sexy."

He lowered his head toward hers, slowly to give her the chance to decide what she wanted. Jane took a deep breath, but she didn't say no. Her eyes said yes. Most definitely yes. She wet her lips.

That was the only invitation he needed.

Chase's mouth pressed against hers fueled by hunger

and need. He needed Jane's kiss as much as he needed air to breathe and water to drink. Her kiss filled him up, yet it wasn't enough. Not nearly enough.

She tasted warm and sweet, like the woman herself.

He kissed the edge of her jawline and nibbled on her ears.

As he wove his fingers through her soft hair, she arched toward him. But it wasn't close enough. He pulled her closer until her soft breasts crushed against him and hot blood roared through his veins.

"Chase," she murmured, her breath warm against his face.

"Do you want me to stop?"

"No," she said. "Please don't."

He captured her lips again. He drank in her sweetness—the taste intoxicating.

Her hands splayed on his back. As her fingers dug into him, the ache inside him grew. Desire battled conscience. Chase struggled to remain in control. He never wanted to let her go. But that wasn't possible.

He pulled away. "It's late. I should take you home."

"I thought I was home."

So did he. And that meant he had a problem. A big problem.

"Soon—" he kissed her lightly on the lips and each corner of her mouth "—you will be."

After an extra long shift at the Hearth and a difficult class complete with pop quiz, Jane couldn't wait to get home. She ate her dinner on the bus ride. She hopped off at her stop and hurried across the street, wondering if Chase had e-mailed her. Not that he said he would. He hadn't said much after driving her home except good night.

Good night, not goodbye.

She touched her lips, remembered the scratchiness of his whiskers against her face.

Okay, now she was being silly. He couldn't say goodbye. They had a benefit to put on. And as for his kisses…

Physical chemistry, that was all. She enjoyed them and so did he. Anything more…

No, Chase might be self-made, and her respect for him increased because of it, but nothing had changed between them. Nothing would. She couldn't get carried away with romantic fantasies and daydreams. Those would get her nowhere.

So what if he'd waited for her outside the theater like an old-fashioned suitor? So what if he'd kissed her with a kind of desperation that both thrilled and frightened her? Kisses didn't mean a man wouldn't change his mind and hit the road once he grew restless or bored. She'd learned that the hard way.

Friends. That's all they were. All they could be.

Jane couldn't afford the consequences of what Chase offered.

On the landing, she unlocked the front door and opened it. The mouthwatering scent of baked cookies filled the air. Michelle always knew what Jane needed. "Hello."

Lamps illuminated the living room and music, The Wiggles if she wasn't mistaken, played on the boom box. But no one answered. It wasn't Emma's bedtime yet. Jane heard a giggle. She followed the sound to the kitchen, entered and froze.

Chase. He was here. Every nerve ending took notice.

Emma stood on a chair next to him at the counter. Together they stirred a large bowl with a wooden spoon. Flour coated every surface, including them, but neither seemed to mind. Warmth blanketed Jane's heart like a hand-stitched quilt passed down through the generations.

"Hi." His grin unleashed a flurry of flutters in her stomach. "How are you?"

"Fine." But she wasn't. He shouldn't be here like this.

He added flour to the bowl. "Not tired, busy or late?"

"Maybe a little tired and late." Seeing him here confused her, yet improved her mood. A lot. "Something smells yummy."

"Cookies." Smudges of white covered Emma's smiling face. "Yummy, yummy, yum."

"So how did you end up here, Chase?" Jane asked.

"I called you, and Michelle answered." He added baking soda to the bowl. "She sounded tired so I offered to play with Emma so she could nap."

Jane's chest squeezed. She should have been here to help.

Emma tilted her chin. "I told Mommy to sleep or she might have to go to the hospital and get poked."

"On my way over—" he dumped salt into the mixture "—I stopped by the store so we would have something to do."

Jane had to give him credit. "An experienced babysitter, huh?"

"No, just an uncle who's helped out in a pinch."

"I don't have an uncle," Emma said. "So he's mine, too."

The guy was a natural with kids, but Jane wondered about his cookie making skills. What was he putting in the bowl?

"So why did you call?" she asked.

"I wanted to talk to you."

The oven buzzed.

Emma clapped. "They're ready."

"Stand back." Chase put on the oven mitt, opened the

oven door and pulled out a tray of round, golden-brown chocolate chip cookies. He used a spatula to move them to a cooling rack.

So much for him not knowing what he was doing. Jane leaned against the doorway. "I'm impressed."

"I told you I could cook."

"It's easy," Emma said. "We opened the package and put the squares on the pan. I helped."

"Shh." Chase touched his index finger to his lips. "That's supposed to be our secret."

Emma placed dough-covered hands over her mouth. "Oops."

Jane laughed. "Don't worry, jelly bean. I kind of suspected something was up."

"Yes, it's okay." Chase mussed Emma's hair. "Jane would have found the wrappers eventually. She's smart."

"My head used to be like a soccer ball," Emma said. "I wanted my hair to grow back purple so it matched Baby, my elephant."

"I like it now." Chase kissed her head. "Very pretty."

"Thank you." Emma beamed. "Your hair is pretty, too."

Jane bit back a chuckle. "If you used premade cookie dough, what's all the mess from?"

"We wanted to at least give the appearance of baking homemade cookies." He tossed a pinch of flour at Emma.

Giggling, she did the same. "Plus it's fun."

Jane retreated as a cookie dough fight ensued. Emma's peals of laughter more than compensated for the mess.

"Aren't you going to join in?" he asked.

Jane spotted the flour in his hand and backed farther away. "No, thanks."

He winked. "You're missing all the fun."

So what else was new? Sometimes she felt like she'd spent her life on the sidelines, observing not participating. "That's okay."

As the flour flew around the kitchen, Jane imagined Chase with children of his own. Smart, cute, healthy kids. An ache throbbed deep within her. Once she'd dreamed of a husband and kids and look where that had got her. She squared her shoulders.

"Time out." Chase made a T with his hands. "The cookies have cooled. Now we can eat them."

He held one out to Emma, but she hesitated. "What time is it, Uncle Chase?"

"Seven-thirty."

She sighed. "I can't have one."

He furrowed his brow. "One cookie?"

"Emma has to take her medicine." Jane hated putting a damper on the fun. "Food can weaken some of the effects of the pills so she can't eat before or after she takes them."

"I'm sorry." He put the cookie back on the cooling rack. "I didn't know."

"It's okay, Uncle Chase." Emma held his hand. "The cookies will still be here tomorrow."

He scooped her up into his arms and hugged her. "Yes, they will, your majesty."

Emma giggled. She touched his nose, leaving a white mark. He did the same to her.

The two of them reminded Jane of her and her father. She wrapped her arms around her trying to dispel the emptiness inside. It didn't help. Tears welled in her eyes, and she rubbed them. Time to get out of here. "Bathtime, jelly bean."

"What's Uncle Chase going to do?" Emma asked.

"Clean up," Jane said.

Emma held her hand. "Are you giving him a bath next?"

"Good question." With a mischievous gleam in his eyes, he leaned back against the counter. "And Uncle Chase would really like to know the answer."

Jane blushed, grabbed a dish towel and threw it at him. "Start cleaning."

CHAPTER EIGHT

CHASE wiped flour from the countertop, not minding the work or the layer of white on his clothes. Seeing the joy on Emma's face was worth having to clean up the mess. And Jane...

If only he could make her laugh the way Emma had. He didn't understand why Jane preferred hanging back and watching. As if life was something to be viewed, not lived. Chase wanted that to change for her.

He scrubbed a chunk of cookie dough from the wall.

"Wow," Emma said, her voice full of awe. "You were wrong, Jane. Uncle Chase can clean."

He glanced over at a blushing Jane. What kind of men had she dated? "Yes, I know how to clean."

"You cook, clean and run a successful company." She laughed. "If I could clone you, I'd be a billionaire."

"But where would that leave me?" he asked.

Her grin reached her eyes, and he felt as if he'd been kicked in the stomach. "In every household in America."

Emma sat at the table. "I have to take my medicine."

Jane removed a pink plastic cup and prescription bottles from an upper cupboard. She filled the cup with water, grabbed a paper towel and carried everything over to the table.

"Okay, Emma." Jane placed different pills on the paper towel. "One at a time."

Emma showed him the first pill. "I'm so happy this isn't the grumpy pill, Uncle Chase. I don't have to take those again until after my treatment."

"Grumpy pills?" he asked.

"Steroids," Jane explained. "They make her grumpy."

Emma swallowed it whole. One by one, she downed the large pills. No complaints, no funny faces, nothing. Chase watched in amazement. He didn't think he could swallow the medicine as easily as she had.

She held the final one. "This is my happy pill."

"Pain medication," Jane said. "They make the pain go away and that makes her happy."

Emma grinned. "All done."

"Great job," he cheered.

"You, too, Uncle Chase," Emma said. "It's really clean in here."

Jane pulled out Emma's chair. "Bedtime, jelly bean."

Emma threw herself against him and hugged tight. Her damp hair smelled like strawberries. "Good night, Uncle Chase."

"Good night, your majesty."

When she let go, Chase felt…odd as if something precious had been stripped from him and he wanted it back.

"I'll just be a minute," Jane said.

As he gave a final wipe to the counters, he sensed a presence behind him and turned.

"Thanks for cleaning the kitchen," she said.

She sounded so damn grateful when he hadn't done much. Did anybody ever help her?

"I made the mess. I should clean it up." He folded the wet rag and placed it in the sparkling sink. "Is Emma in bed?"

"She decided to sleep with Michelle tonight," Jane said. "Both mommy and daughter are on their way to dreamland."

"Michelle's lucky to have you for a friend."

"I'm lucky to have her," Jane admitted. "Michelle helped me make it through some tough times."

"Your dad?"

Jane nodded. "I took care of him when he got sick and he wasn't as good a patient as Emma."

He sat at the table. "What about your mom?"

"She died when I was a baby."

"I'm sorry." Chase hurt for her. "That must have been hard taking care of your dad on your own."

Jane shrugged. "I did what had to be done."

No doubt she threw herself into the task wholeheartedly. Just like she did with everything else. She probably put her life on hold and never complained once. The more Chase learned about her, the more he respected her. Appreciated her, too. Not many people were as giving as Jane Dawson.

He thought about the time, three years ago, when he'd been lying in a hospital bed, bruised and broken after a climbing accident. He'd been dating Sierra, a vivacious and beautiful model, for longer than normal, and wondered if he should give the settling down thing a try. That was until he overheard her talking to her girlfriend when she thought he was asleep and discovered Sierra planned to take care of him only if she had full access to his bank account.

Chase can even climb again once I get the ring on my finger and the will rewritten.

He'd never been head over heels about Sierra, but her words still hurt. So did his ego for not realizing her true motivation sooner.

"Your father was a lucky man to have you as a daughter," Chase said. "Tell me about him."

"He was a great dad." Jane took two cookies from the cookie rack, gave Chase one and sat at the table. "For years he worked at a restaurant in Southeast Portland. He had a stable job with full benefits, but he wanted more. He told me you had to risk big, to win big."

"A man after my own heart."

She broke her cookie in half. "You remind me a little of him sometimes. One day he decided to put it all on the line and open his own café."

"What happened?"

"It was going well until he got sick and was diagnosed with cancer. He had no medical insurance, no disability pay and no one to help him out. He lost everything."

"But he gave it a shot."

"That's what my dad said until the very end." She got a faraway look in her eyes. She blinked, and Chase thought she might cry, but no tears fell. "He never would admit that opening the café probably killed him. If he'd had medical insurance he would have gone to the doctor sooner. Maybe they could have caught it…"

"What-ifs can drive you crazy." Chase spoke from experience. He'd stumbled at the beginning with Cyberworx, tangled in a spiderweb of second-guessing before he achieved any measurable success. "They can't change what happened."

"No, nothing can," Jane said. "But you can make sure you don't repeat the same mistakes."

"I take it you're not much of a risk-taker."

"No, I'm not," she admitted. "I'm…cautious."

Jane did carry her own scars. Those kept her, at first, from believing she could organize the fundraiser, Chase realized. And from understanding how amazing she was as a person. She needed to take a risk and succeed. She needed to…live again.

"Would you try something a little adventurous with me?" he asked.

She crumbled her last piece of cookie into bits. "Is it dangerous?"

"I won't let anything happen to you."

Jane pursed her lips. "You didn't answer my question."

"Some people might consider it dangerous."

"Then no," she said quickly. "I don't do danger. I'm addicted to breathing."

"Aren't we all?"

"Sometimes I wonder."

He laughed. "If you do this with me, I'll do whatever you want in return."

She leaned forward. "Whatever I want?"

"Yes." This would be a way to repay her for all she'd done for Emma and the benefit. Not to mention him. She'd treated him to lunch twice, coffee, pastries. "Dinner, a shopping spree, spa day, you name it. On me."

"Michelle can't get the time off so I'm taking Emma to the clinic for her next treatment. Would you come with us?"

Chase struggled to understand. He had offered Jane so much more. "That's all you want in return?"

She nodded. "It's during the week so you'd miss some work, but it would mean so much to Emma to have you there with us."

Strange. All Jane desired was his time. Even when he offered her carte blanche, she asked only for his help and for someone else, never herself. "I'll go with you."

"Thanks."

"No, thank you." He leaned back in his chair. "You're going to like what I have in mind for you, Jane. You're going to like it very much."

On Thursday evening, Jane's concerns over Chase's plans for her disappeared. She stared at the boxy building. What could be dangerous inside a health club? A killer stair climber, a rogue cycling machine, a kickass aerobics class? No doubt she was getting the better end of this bargain.

"I saw that. A smile." Chase stood in front of a pair of glass doors wearing a pair of ratty sweatpants and a T-shirt. The exercise clothes made him look younger, more carefree, and she didn't feel out of place in her leggings and T-shirt. "Does this mean you're ready?"

"Ready as I'll ever be."

He opened one of the doors. "Let's go then."

Jane walked inside. The place resembled a hotel with its big front desk and atrium filled with plants. A young woman wearing a blond ponytail, a black warm-up suit and a big smile greeted them and asked Jane to sign in.

"This way," Chase said when she'd finished.

"So what are we going to do?" She followed him around the corner into a big area with a huge rock wall at least three stories tall. Maybe six. Multicolored tape hung from the rocks. The carpeted floor seemed padded—at least she hoped it was—and music played through speakers. But not even the familiar song put her at ease. She gulped.

"Come on," Chase urged.

Jane took a step back. "I've changed my mind."

He held her hand and squeezed. "You can do this."

Chase didn't understand. Jane rarely strayed from the tried and tested path. Searching him out had been the biggest risk she'd taken in years. "I can't."

"Yes, you can."

Jane couldn't. She set realistic goals and hedged her bets against Fate. Control. She needed to be in control. But up on the wall, the only thing in control was gravity. "I'm sorry."

"If you don't like it, you can stop."

"I—"

"Hey, mate." A good-looking guy with muscled arms and a thick Australian accent interrupted them. He wore the gym's black uniform. "Are you going with the club to Smith Rock?"

Chase rubbed the scar above his eye. "I stick to walls now, Nathan."

"Sorry, mate, I forgot." He gave Jane the once-over and smiled. "I'm Nathan Tyler. What can I do for you?"

"A harness and shoes for my friend," Chase answered.

Interest gleamed in Nathan's eyes. "Just a friend?"

"To you she will be," Chase said, the warning clear in her voice.

He sounded jealous. Jane bit back a smile. "I can decide my own friends. Thank you very much."

"A woman who thinks for herself." Nathan winked. "I like that."

Chase glowered at her, sat on a nearby bench and removed his sneakers.

"Shoe size, love?" Nathan asked.

"Eight."

"Ever climb before?"

"No."

"Don't worry." He handed her a pair of shoes and a harness. "You're in good hands with Chase. The guy might be a cutthroat businessman, but he's one of the best climbers around. Even better since the accident. He's taught me a thing or two."

Accident? That might explain the scar. "Thanks."

Too bad Nathan's words didn't make her feel any better. As she sat on the bench, Chase rose and removed his sweatpants. Underneath he wore tight shorts similar to what cyclists wore. Her mouth went dry. She tried not to stare.

He joined her on the bench. "He's not your type."

"Who?"

"Nathan." Chase put on a shoe. "He's a ladies' man."

She felt an unfamiliar rush of feminine power. "I know."

"Then why did you say—?"

"Because of what you said." She tied her climbing shoes—a tighter fit than her sneakers. "I'm a big girl, Chase. I don't need anyone looking out for me."

His gaze met hers. "But wouldn't it be nice if someone did look after you?"

"Are you volunteering for the job?"

He didn't answer.

"Didn't think so." She touched the jagged scar above his

eye, the skin rough beneath her fingertip. "What happened?"

"I was climbing."

"Climbing?"

He nodded. "Not here. On a mountain. I...fell."

She glanced at the wall and a shiver inched down her spine. "Was it a bad fall?"

"Depends on your definition of bad."

"Please tell me."

"I had a head injury, was in a coma and woke up."

Oh, boy. She didn't want to do this. She crossed her arms over her chest. "You could have died."

"But I didn't. I survived." He tied his other shoe. "I learned from the experience and wouldn't ask you to do this if I didn't know you could do it."

He might believe she could do this, but she didn't.

"Trust me." He stood and reached out his hand.

The decision was hers. She took a deep breath and took hold of his hand.

He pulled her to her feet. "Time for your harness."

She stepped into a harness that wrapped around her thighs. Having Chase assist her was awkward. His hand kept brushing her thighs and hips. Heated sensations shot outward from the spots he touched. Thank goodness she hadn't worn shorts. At least she could pretend she had some composure.

"You'll be attached to a rope," he said. "I'll belay you."

"What does that mean?" she asked.

"I'll hold onto the rope." He attached the rope to the harness. "I won't let you fall."

Her necked ached from staring up the wall. "It's too high."

Chase smiled. "Which is why we're going to start over here. The different colors of tape mark the various routes, but they don't dictate difficulty."

"So how do you know which is easiest or harder?"

"Experience, plus the white tape will tell you this is a beginner route." He pointed to a 5.7 marker. "That's the degree of difficulty."

"It looks difficult to me."

"This is called a hold." Ignoring her, he pointed to a palm-size rock screwed onto the wall. "You can hold on with your fingers or step on them with your feet. Try it."

She did. Not a lot to hold onto.

"The key is to only move one ligament at a time."

"Ligament?" she asked.

"Hand or foot," he explained. "Body position is key. Balance on your feet."

"I'll never remember everything." Especially with him standing so close to her.

"I'm here to help you. You can do this, Jane."

He might think so, but she still had doubts. And fear. A whole lot of fear.

"Here's some chalk." He opened a small pouch hanging around his waist and pulled out a ball. "Rub this around your hands."

As she rolled the ball with her palms, a layer of chalk covered her hands. She gave him the ball and he put it in the bag.

"Let's go."

She stepped up with one foot and reached with her hand. He stood behind her shadowing her moves. With his body touching her backside she could barely breathe let alone move.

He touched her arms and legs. "Stay close to the wall."

Having his hands on her felt good. Intimate. She tried to focus, hard to do with the heat emanating from him. Strength, too. But if she didn't concentrate, she would fall.

"As you climb, I'll pull the rope. Nothing will happen to you." He squeezed her shoulder. "Trust me, okay?"

She had no choice but to trust him. Well, he'd given her the choice, but she'd made a bargain with him. And oddly, her urge not to disappoint him was stronger than her fears right now. She reached with one hand.

"Now move your hand to the next hold," he instructed.

She did. "This isn't so bad."

"Keep going," he encouraged. "Climbing is like a dance. If you get your footwork mixed up, you have problems."

"And if you don't?"

"Then you can't wait to do it again."

Jane doubted that, but, at least, she was overcoming her fear of dying tonight. The higher she climbed, the more her arms throbbed. She stopped and clung to the wall. "I can't go any higher. My forearms feel like they are going to explode."

"They're super pumped," Chase said. "It's normal."

Nothing about this was normal. "I want to stop."

"Before you do, take a deep breath."

She did and looked down. Uh-oh. "I'm going to fall."

"I won't let you fall," he said. "Focus on my voice. My words. And keep looking up."

She cleared her mind. Tried to at least.

"Move your right hand."

Jane did and followed each of his instructions. A rhythm developed. And when he stopped talking, she continued up the wall. "I'm doing it."

"Yes, you are," he yelled. "You're dancing, Jane."

She was dancing. Pride rushed through her. She kept going, though her arms burned and she couldn't feel her fingers. She reached the top. "Yes."

Jane couldn't remember feeling such exhilaration or such a sense of accomplishment before. She wanted to stay up there. But under Chase's direction, she rappelled to the gym floor. Doing so was as much fun as the climb had been.

She shook her hands. Blood rushed. Her forearms remained swollen. Her fingers wouldn't flex. She'd lost all strength in them.

"Great job," he said.

Jane hugged him. Well, at least tried given the state of her arms. She kissed his cheek. "Thank you."

"For what?"

"For believing I could do this when I didn't."

He laughed. "You did this on your own."

Well, with his assistance. Still she was the one who had climbed the wall. It had been scary and fun. Not deadly.

Thanks to Chase.

Her fears didn't limit her when he was around. Worry and anxiety no longer ruled her. Chase helped her feel safe and confident, whether she was standing next to him or thirty feet up a rock wall. And that made Jane feel good, better than she had in years.

Maybe it was time to take a few chances. She glanced at Chase and smiled. Maybe it was time to try a new dance.

CHAPTER NINE

THE next week dragged. The MFR merger exploded. Chase worked at the office from six in the morning until ten at night to salvage the deal. It didn't help that the benefit was less than three weeks away. He spent too many hours on the phone checking details at the winery, tracking down guests and trying to live up to his promise to Jane. He'd barely seen her this week, but thoughts of her drifted into his mind a dozen times a day.

Sitting at his desk, Chase studied the Cyberworx P&L statement for last quarter. The numbers blurred. He dropped his pen and rubbed his tired eyes.

Once the benefit was over, his workload would lighten, but his excuse to see Jane would also disappear. He hadn't figured out what to do about that. The attraction between them burned too strong from them to be only friends, yet they weren't dating. Sure they spent time together, but except for Jane's peck on his cheek at the rock wall, they hadn't kissed again.

He wanted to kiss her. He liked kissing her. But kisses seemed to complicate things, so they avoided the issue like two parachutists about to jump but refusing to step out of the plane.

Not that he was unhappy about it. Why ruin a good thing?

He enjoyed being with Jane whether they were working on the benefit, watching a DVD with Emma or just talking. They'd grown comfortable with each other, had developed a real rapport.

So…no more kisses. He could live with that. Couldn't he?

As long as he didn't see her too often or touch her at all or think about her too much…

He refocused on the spreadsheet in front of him.

"Boss?" Amanda walked into his office, carrying a handful of papers. "Tiffany Trimble from the *Willamette Journal* called. She wants an interview."

"Have public relations handle it." He didn't look up. "I don't have time."

"She wants to write about the Once Upon A Time benefit."

Damn. Taking more time from his busy schedule to talk to a reporter was the last thing he wanted to do, but the free publicity would bring more people to the event. "I'll do it."

"She would like to speak with you and Jane Dawson."

Jane.

She'd come a long way in the brief time they'd known each other. He'd known she had it in her, but watching her confidence blossom and seeing her handle the responsibilities of the benefit made him proud. She could handle the interview, no doubt. But he wanted to ask her first because they were in this together. It wouldn't be right to make the decision for her.

"Let me to speak with Jane first and I'll let you know what to say to Ms. Trimble."

"Whatever you say, boss." Amanda's eyes twinkled. "Or maybe in this case, whatever Jane says."

Chase grimaced. "Get out."

"This is great." On a break at the Hearth, Jane raised the empty wineglass to the light. The words Ryder Estate Winery were etched on the front. "Do you like how it came out?"

"I do." Chase removed his black sports jacket and placed it on the back of his chair. He loosened his tie and pushed up the sleeves of the dress shirt he wore. "And putting a boxed chocolate truffle in each glass will be a great touch."

"Thanks. Check this out." Delighted their ideas meshed, Jane removed a small piece of ivory cardstock from her apron pocket. It had a black and white picture of Emma dressed up like a princess with the words Once Upon A Time… written in script. On the bottom of the card was a blank space for a guest's name. "Kendra, one of the baristas who's studying graphic design, created it."

"It's perfect."

"The print shop offered to donate the paper and the copying. All we'll have to do is put the guests' names on the cards, hole punch them and tie them on the stems of each glass."

"That's all?"

"Don't worry." Jane placed the card against the glass stem to see how it would look. Perfect. He was right again. "It won't be that bad."

"Easy for you to say," he said. "Look at my fingers. Try to tie ribbon with these things."

"I've seen bigger."

Amusement glinted in his eyes. "Oh, really."

She nodded. "But I won't make you tie on the cards."

He frowned. "I'm not letting you do it all yourself."

Chase had been swamped at Cyberworx, but she appreciated how he made sure she didn't have to carry all the workload. He'd said he wanted to be a part of the fundraiser and he'd come through, in more ways than one. Jane smiled.

"I won't be tying them, either." She motioned to the counter. "My crew offered to help with the wineglasses and also handle check-in at the event."

He raised his frothy latte. "It's all coming together."

"Two more weeks."

And then it would be over. Her and Chase, too? Mixed feelings surged through her.

"Speaking of which, I wanted to talk to you."

About them perhaps? A chill rushed through her. "What?"

"A reporter wants to write an article on the benefit."

"Great." This was the final piece they needed. They'd done flyers, contacted civic and church groups and Chase had hit up every mover and shaker in town, but they hadn't received much interest from the media. Jane leaned forward. "The publicity will help ticket sales. We have room for around fifty more, and people who don't want to attend could still send in donations if the newspaper will help us out with that."

He grinned, and her pulse quickened. "I'm glad you agree because the reporter wants to interview both of us."

Jane stiffened. She'd never done an interview before.

"They'll probably send a photographer and want photos of Emma, too," he said. "Is that okay?"

Niggling doubts crept in, but Jane pushed them away.

The publicity would help Emma's benefit. That's what mattered. Jane no longer felt inadequate or insecure. If she could climb a rock wall, she could face a reporter and photographer. "I'll do it. I'm sure Michelle will agree, too."

His grin widened, reaching his eyes. "I'll have Amanda set it up for us."

Us.

Jane liked hearing him say that word. It didn't mean anything. Not really. But she cared for Chase. She appreciated his help. She enjoyed being with him.

And she didn't want any of that to change.

On Saturday, Jane recounted the boxes of wineglasses that had been delivered to the barn. She was in too good a mood to let anything worry her. The event was coming together. She felt giddy with pride and relief. "We have too many glasses."

"I ordered extras for the winery." Chase looked much too handsome in his brown sweater and tan pants. "I might open the winery to the public for a holiday tasting."

"You should do it." She'd gotten to know the winery staff over the past few weeks. "It would give your employees here the opportunity to show off what they've accomplished."

"Good point."

She grinned. "That's why I brought it up."

"A little cocky, but cute."

Jane stuck out her tongue at him. "Takes one to know one."

"You're going to pay for that." He circled around a box, heading right for her.

"Only if you can catch me."

She dashed through the barn. Chase raced after her, caught her and picked her up in his arms.

Heart pounding, breathless with laughter and more than ready for another kiss, she wet her lips. "What are you going to do with me?"

He smirked. "Wouldn't you like to know?"

His suggestive tone sent a burst of heat rushing through her. So did his hands around her. "You could put me down."

"I don't think so."

"You could steal me away to your castle like a dark lord."

"Not exactly what I had in mind."

"What did you have in mind?" she asked.

"This." He slung her over his shoulder like a sack of potatoes. "What do you think?"

Maybe if he moved his hand up a little… No, she couldn't suggest that. They were here to work, not play. Still there was nothing wrong with having a little fun. "I would have preferred being carried like Scarlett O'Hara up the stairs."

"I'm no Rhett Butler."

"No, but I didn't realize you were the caveman type."

He squeezed her thigh. "Be careful what you say, Jane Dawson, or I might drop you."

She knew he wouldn't, but she played along.

Chase carried her outside and down a cobblestone path. Uncomfortable and surprisingly turned on, Jane didn't squirm. She was too busy enjoying the view from this angle. He had a nice butt.

He strode down a green hillside and stopped. A breeze ruffled her hair. She could almost taste the scent of freshly mowed grass. He placed his hands on her waist, lifted her up and set her on her feet in front of him.

She stared up at him. Gray clouds covered the overcast autumn sky, but a patch of blue attempted to break through.

"Turn around," he said.

Jane didn't want to turn. She wanted to kiss him.

"Please."

She did and gasped. A picnic basket overflowing with food and wine sat on top of a large yellow blanket spread over the grass. "Wow."

With a satisfied smile on his face, he reached inside the basket. A slow jazzy tune played from inside. An iPod or MP3 player, she wondered.

"This is great. Incredible." She knew Chase barely had time to sleep these days, much less arrange a lovely picnic for her. His efforts touched her. "But you shouldn't have gone to so much trouble."

"I wanted to. You've been working so hard and you fed me lunch," he said. "I figured it was my turn."

Her lunches had sandwiches and soup. This felt more like a date. But no date she'd ever been on. Overwhelmed, she sank to the blanket. "Thanks."

He sat next to her. His leg brushed hers sending a burst of tingles through her. "And we haven't spent that much time together lately."

Her heart leaped. Jane shouldn't read too much into his words, but she had a hard time believing he would have done this for any old friend. "You've been busy."

"So have you. We deserve a break. I thought this would be fun."

"It looks like fun to me."

"Eleanor Roosevelt once said 'Yesterday is past. Tomorrow is mystery. Today is a gift.'" He uncorked a bottle, poured the red wine into glasses and handed one to Jane. "Here's to enjoying the gift of today."

She tapped her glass against his and sipped. "Delicious."

"Yes, it is." He took a sip, but his eyes never strayed from her mouth. "Look at the bottle."

The label had the same black and white picture of Emma dressed as a princess with the words Once Upon A Time, Private Reserve and the date of the event printed on it. "How did you do this?"

"Kendra. I talked to her after I saw the cards she designed for the wineglasses." He placed the bottle in the basket and pulled out a plate with a baguette, knife and cheese on it. "She wanted a wine label for her graphic design class portfolio."

"It's great." Jane ate a piece of Havarti cheese. "Why did you continue with the winery when you bought this place? You didn't have to go into the wine business."

"No, but it's always been a dream of mine," he admitted. "When I was younger, my parents would open a bottle of wine on holidays. They couldn't really afford it other times of the year. We would each get our own glass filled with an ounce or so of wine and my father would make a toast. I remember my mother saying she wished we could do this more often and I told her someday I would have my own winery so she could have a bottle of wine whenever she wanted."

"That's so sweet." Each revelation about Chase's life increased her curiosity about him. She imagined him as a young boy, with his curly hair and easy smile. He must have been adorable. "You're a good son."

Chase shrugged.

"Any other dreams you have now?" Jane asked.

He stretched out his legs in front of him. "I'd like to make some changes to my foundation."

She had expected him to mention something about Cyberworx or making the Forbes 400. "What kind of changes?"

"I'd like to work with those in need rather than just throwing money at a problem." He gazed into her eyes and goose bumps covered her arms. "Organizing Emma's benefit has taught me how important being involved is. It's a bigger commitment, but more fulfilling. I didn't understand what I was missing until I met you. So, thank you."

"You're welcome." His words gave her such peace and satisfaction. But they also gave her courage. To find out more about this special man. "What about a family?"

He choked on his wine. "A family of my own?"

"Yes."

"I almost considered it once, around the time of the climbing accident."

"What happened?" Jane asked.

"The woman I was seeing was more in love with my bank account then me."

He sounded amused, not bitter. Still she imagined how much that must have hurt him. "I'm sorry."

"Don't be." He took a drink. "Finding out the truth was the best thing that ever happened to me."

"Yes, but the truth isn't always easy to hear."

His gaze locked on hers. "You sound as if you speak from experience."

She nodded. "I had a boyfriend. We were sort of engaged. He hadn't bought the ring, and we hadn't set the date."

The more Jane said, the more pathetic it sounded.

"What happened?" Chase asked.

"My father got sick. My transformation from college student to caretaker didn't quite fit into my boyfriend's plans. He got bored and moved to Seattle."

"The guy must have been an idiot. A real loser."

Jane laughed. "Let's just say he was self-centered. I know now it never would have worked out. I was young and may have been more enamored of the idea of getting married than being with him."

A hawk flew overhead. He refilled her wineglass. "So I told you mine. It's time you told me yours."

"My what?"

"Your dreams."

"I want to earn my college degree. I would like to run my own coffee house. And someday I want to create a fund to help other uninsured leukemia patients."

He raised his glass to her. "Those are worthy dreams."

"More like goals."

"Either way," he said. "I have no doubt you'll be able to achieve them all, Jane."

Two months ago, she would have disagreed with him, claiming that if she clung to unrealistic expectations she would only be disappointed. But things had changed. From the beginning, Chase had believed in her abilities. He'd shown her what faith in herself could accomplish.

When she was with Chase, Jane felt like she was soaring, flying so high she never wanted to come down to the ground. She felt safe, confident, pretty. She could do anything she wanted with his encouragement. His support. His love.

Her heart pounded. She took a sip of wine. It didn't help.

Jane couldn't deny it any longer. She had a dream, a big one. Chase.

She'd never felt this way about anyone before, had never trusted anyone the way she trusted him. He'd come through on every promise he'd made to her. They'd learned to rely on each other, as partners and friends, and doing so opened up parts of herself she'd hidden away.

She was falling for him, falling hard.

He was drawn to her, too, she could tell. He tried so hard to please her, like surprising her with this picnic, but simply being with him was enough.

"Yesterday is past," she reminded herself of Eleanor Roosevelt's words. "Tomorrow is a mystery. Today is a gift."

Jane made up her mind to enjoy it.

He missed her.

As Chase wrestled day and night over the details of the MFR merger, he didn't want to admit how much. Maybe he should have kissed Jane at the picnic.

She had been playful and happy, sitting on that yellow blanket, eating food and drinking wine. Everything felt so right, so easy, and he'd wanted to reach over and take her in his arms.

Then again, maybe it was a good thing he hadn't kissed her. He wasn't about to be the next guy who broke her overburdened heart. Plus she'd told him her dreams: *I want to earn my college degree. I would like to run my own coffee house. And someday I want to create a fund to help other uninsured leukemia patients.*

Too bad she hadn't mentioned a hit-and-run romance with a commitment-shy mogul as one of her goals. But she hadn't. So he held back. He liked her too well, admired her too much, to ask her to accept less than what she wanted. That didn't mean he couldn't continue to see her for the right reasons.

When the day of Emma's treatment arrived, Chase picked them up. Seeing Emma sitting in her booster seat in the back of his car was a little strange, as if they were playing house. The three of them almost seemed like they were a family. That the notion didn't terrify him was unsettling.

While Jane and Emma signed in, Chase sat in one of the comfortable chairs and checked out the waiting area of the pediatric oncology clinic. The kid-friendly space had an aquarium full of fish and a shelf with books and magazines.

Across from him sat a woman who looked like she'd been to hell and back that day. She rocked a small baby wrapped in a blue and yellow blanket. Tears glistened in her dark-circled eyes and she muttered the words to a familiar prayer.

A young toddler, so pale the purple bruises on her face appeared painted on, lay almost limp across her mother's lap. The woman kept her lips pressed together and never took her eyes off the little girl.

A bald boy, about the same size as Chase's five-year-old niece, sat on the floor at a man's feet and dug through a backpack filled with toys. The man held a magazine, but his attention was clearly focused on the boy.

Chase thought about Jane asking him about wanting a family of his own. He'd never really answered her question. He couldn't. He had a happy childhood. He had a great family. But he still saw himself as the good son, the fun-loving brother, the silly uncle. He didn't want that to change. He wasn't ready for the kind of responsibility facing him in this waiting room. Surrounded by sick children and anxious parents, he wasn't sure how to feel, how to act.

He read a magazine cover, but didn't pick it up. His attention strayed to the children around him, but he tried not to stare. It was all could do not to call P.J. at the foundation and triple the donations made to various children's charities this year, but that didn't seem enough for these kids.

Emma bounced over to the little girl on her mommy's lap. "Hello, Bebe."

But Bebe didn't say a word. She didn't move. Jane whispered in Emma's ear and led her over. The little girl smiled. "Did you see the fish, Uncle Chase?"

"I did." He couldn't believe how unaffected Emma seemed here. She acted as if everything she saw was completely normal. Maybe for her, it was. "I didn't know Nemo lived here."

"Yes, and Dori, too." Emma pointed to the blue tang fish immortalized by the movie *Finding Nemo*. "All they do is swim, swim, swim."

"What's the basket of hats for?" Chase asked.

Emma's eyes widened. "You get to take one for free."

"After certain chemo treatments, hair falls out," Jane explained.

He knew that. But these were kids and he just didn't think…

That was the problem. Until meeting Jane, Michelle and Emma, Chase hadn't given a moment's consideration to what sick children went through each day as they battled cancer or other life-threatening illnesses.

A nurse called out Bebe's name and her mother carried her back.

"We usually have to wait fifteen to thirty minutes," Jane said.

"I'm not worried about the time," he said. "They aren't expecting me back at the office today."

Surprise registered in her eyes.

"I didn't know whether you would need me to get food or something for Emma," he explained.

The happy glow on Jane's face could light the Las Vegas strip. It surely lit his day. "Thank you. For taking time off and for coming here. It's…great."

A warm feeling rushed through him. Jane acted as if his presence alone was a special gift. He felt unbelievably grateful for her undeserved attention.

Emma climbed onto his lap and she laid her head on his shoulder. Her small, lightweight body seeming almost fragile. She smelled sweet like a mixture of strawberries and cotton candy. "I'm glad you're here, too."

"I am, too." Chase wanted to know Jane better, to figure out what drove her. Being here might give him a glimpse into what she endured with her father.

"My friend Mariah used to come here," Emma said. "We would play. But Mariah doesn't come here now. She's in Heaven. What do you think she's doing in Heaven right now, Uncle Chase?"

She stared up at him with genuine interest, the look in her eyes making her seem older.

Chase prided himself on having all the answers, but this one stumped him. How could he explain Heaven to a four-year-old when he'd barely contemplated it himself?

"That's a good question, jelly bean." Jane brushed her fingers through Emma's soft hair. "What do you think she's doing?"

"I don't know that's why I asked."

"Do you remember how much Mariah loved flowers?" Jane prompted.

"I do," Emma said. "She could be bouncing on the flowers."

"I'm sure Mariah would love doing that."

Emma's mouth formed a small O. "Do you think Slayter is bouncing with her, too?"

He had no idea who Slayter was, but he could guess. No child should have to lose so many friends at such a young age. Chase glanced around the room at the other children. Some of them might not survive. Even Emma…

A lump formed in his throat. He held onto her tighter.

"What do you think, Emma?" Jane asked softly, as if they were discussing a ride at the playground not the afterlife.

"I think they are playing together and bouncing on flowers." Emma sighed. "I miss them."

The pure and raw emotion in her young voice hit Chase hard. His eyes stung, and he rubbed them. He needed to do more. Fund research. Help families. Educate others.

Jane caressed Emma's cheek. "I know you do, jelly bean."

And Jane did. One of Chase's strengths lay in his ability to recognize where his employees' skills would be utilized best. He knew without a doubt the perfect position for Jane Dawson—wife and mother. Oh sure, she could find success doing whatever else she wanted, but Jane would thrive with her own husband and children. The idea, both compelling and frightening, wrapped itself around him.

Emma pouted. "I want my mommy."

Jane rubbed Emma's head. "I know you do, but

remember she has to work. That's why Uncle Chase came. It takes two of us to make up for one mommy. Okay?"

She nodded.

"Emma Taylor," a nurse called. The little girl hopped off his lap and ran to the woman whose nametag read Rachel. "Let's see how much you've grown since the last time you were here."

Rachel weighed and measured Emma then checked her blood pressure and temperature. "Now it's time to go to your room."

On the way, Chase stepped around a tricycle in the hallway. The private room looked like a normal examining room except for the pillows and blankets on the exam bed.

"I'll be right back," Rachel said.

Jane sat on the bed and Emma climbed onto her lap. As Jane told a story about a purple elephant, she unbuttoned Emma's shirt.

Rachel returned. "All set, kiddo?"

Emma nodded.

The nurse eyed Chase. "You're new to this."

Was it that apparent? "Yes. I'm a friend of the family."

"He's my uncle Chase."

"Emma has a port-a-cath in her chest. We use that for drawing blood and infusing medicine. At home they put numbing cream around the area and taped it. I'm going to remove the tape now." Rachel gave a quick pull. "Now I'll wipe off the cream and access the port so I can draw blood."

"Is it okay if I don't watch?" he asked.

Emma laughed. "You are funny, Uncle Chase."

It wouldn't be funny if he passed out. This wasn't a place for the faint of heart. He stared at the tiled floor.

The nurse finished, and Emma selected a prize from the treasure chest—a pink bracelet.

"We'll have the results soon."

As the minutes passed, Jane didn't take her eyes off the door. She kept a smile on her face, but the look in her eyes was anything but relaxed.

He placed his hand on her shoulders. "You okay?"

"I'll feel better after we get the blood results," she said, her voice low. "You never know how they'll turn out."

Emma played with her bracelet. If she was aware of any concern or problems, she gave no sign.

He wrapped his arm around Jane, and she leaned against him. Holding her felt so natural. Natural and right. But he hated the reason she was in his arms again was fear and worry.

A knock sounded on the door. Dr. Kempler, an energetic blonde in her forties, welcomed them warmly. She spoke with Emma first then turned to Jane. "Emma's results look good."

"Thank goodness," she muttered, her relief palpable.

The doctor smiled. "We'll do the spinal tap first."

They went to a procedure room that looked like a small operating room. The anesthesiologist, Dr. Liu, asked Jane questions about Emma's medication history and reactions to being put to sleep. The multisyllable medical terms sounded like a foreign language to Chase so he kept Emma entertained with finger shadows while they connected blood and oxygen readers.

"Now I'm going to get my sleepy medicine, Uncle Chase."

Emma was all smiles as Jane held her and Dr. Liu put medication into the catheter line. Within three seconds,

Emma was sound asleep, a real life Sleeping Beauty. With gentleness and love, Jane laid her on the bed.

Chase stared mesmerized. Seeing this nurturing side to Jane shouldn't have surprised him. He'd known how giving she was and thought she'd make a great wife and mother. Yet his world suddenly tilted on its axis because now he not only imagined Jane as a mother, but as the mother of his children.

An aching void enveloped him. He'd thought his life was complete, that he had all he wanted. But for one dizzying moment, he considered what he could be missing and it rammed his heart like a lightning bolt.

"Come on," she said.

Her words startled him. "We leave Emma alone?"

"The doctors prefer we do," Jane said. "It's okay. She's off having euphoric dreams right now and won't know. Kids love the sleepy medicine."

"Can't we stay?" He couldn't explain why, but he was hesitant to leave Emma. Misguided responsibility? Fear? He just knew he didn't want to leave her.

"We'll wait right outside the door." Jane placed her hand on his shoulder. It was all he could do not to pull her against him and not let go. "It'll be fine. We're only getting started with the appointment. Emma still has two infusions."

"It's a long appointment."

"It's much longer when something is wrong with her numbers," Jane said. "But it's always harder on Emma when Michelle can't make an appointment."

"You would never know it today."

"That's because her uncle Chase is with her."

"Me?" he asked.

"Yes, you."

The tenderness in Jane's eyes tugged at his heart. "I had no idea what to expect, but I'm glad I'm here.

"I'm happy you're here, too."

The ache in him intensified. His affection for Jane grew every time he saw her, but this felt different, deeper and he wasn't quite sure what to make of the emotion. Nor was he sure what he should do about it.

Or, Chase realized, Jane.

CHAPTER TEN

THE NIGHT BEFORE the interview, not a single item remained hanging in Jane's closet. Clothing lay strewn on her floor and piled on her bed. Nervous about the interview and excited to see Chase again, she couldn't decide what to wear.

Nothing seemed right so she'd called in the closest things to fashionistas in her life—Michelle and Ally—to help. Emma wanted to add her opinion, too, and wanted Jane to wear a sparkly plastic tiara. It spoke volumes about her life when she needed fashion advice from a thirty-something single mom, a twenty-something barista and a four-year-old.

"I have another crown," Emma said. "I'll get it."

"I like the brown outfit," Michelle said. "The one Zoe dropped off with the short skirt and cute jacket."

"I agree, except ditch the pink blouse." Ally tossed a pale green shirt to Jane. "Try this one instead."

"Green?" Jane asked.

"It matches your eyes." Ally nodded. "Add Michelle's beaded necklace and earrings and you'll look hot."

Jane remembered the way Chase watched her at the clinic. His gaze hungry and adoring at the same time. She wanted him to look at her that way again. Who was she kidding? She wanted him to kiss her. Maybe a little hotness wouldn't hurt. "I do need to be taken seriously."

"You will be," Michelle said. "And Chase still won't be able to resist you."

"Don't forget I'm doing this for the interview." Jane put on the blouse. "The one to publicize Emma's benefit."

"Sure you are." Ally winked.

Michelle nodded. "Keep telling yourself that, sweetie."

"I will." Jane buttoned up the shirt. The clinging fabric revealed her curves. "But I wouldn't mind if Chase noticed I cleaned up well."

Ally nodded. "He'll notice more than that."

Michelle grinned. "Most definitely."

Jane hoped so. She wanted Chase to see her as more than his event-planning partner and friend. She wanted him to see how far she had come over these past weeks. She wanted him to find her irresistible.

"So are we talking lust or love?" Ally asked.

"Love," Michelle said, her voice wistful.

"Let's not get carried away." At least not yet. Jane put on the jacket. "Chase and I are friends. We respect each other. We haven't had time for anything else." Well, unless you counted three mind-blowing, heart-melting kisses.

Ally snickered. "Let's hope he respects you, because he's not going to be able to keep his hands off you."

Trouble was, Chase had been a perfect gentleman since that night at the theater. Jane could do with a little less respect from him if it meant he'd kiss her again. She adjusted the hem of the jacket. "How do I look?"

"Fantastic."

"Gorgeous."

"Hot," they said together.

Emma ran back into the room. She held a purple crown. "You look pretty."

Jane took a deep breath. She only hoped Chase agreed.

The interview had to be done, but Chase wasn't looking forward to it. Not when that meant spending more time with Jane. She'd already taken over his thoughts and dreams. Wife and mother. Mother and wife. Nothing stilled the images of building a life with her. And he wanted—no needed—them to stop.

Jane climbed out of a red Escort. She waved goodbye to a blonde—Ally from the Hearth if he wasn't mistaken— and turned toward him. His breath caught in his throat.

Her suit looked professional, but approachable. Not to mention sexy with the above the knee skirt and fitted jacket. The layers of her new haircut framed her face and accentuated her high cheekbones. But the confidence in her posture, the determined set of her chin and self-assured smile on her face were what made him stare. "You are so beautiful."

Not the most indifferent words he could have said, but his compliment brought a flush to her cheeks. "My boss Zoe loaned me the outfit."

"I doubt they look as good on her."

"Don't let her hear you say that." Jane's eyes, the color magnified by her green shirt, twinkled behind her glasses. "I don't want to get fired."

"I'd hire you."

"To do what?"

"I can think of several positions I'd want you in."

She raised a brow. "Such as?"

His temperature rose at the images forming in his mind. Wife and mother, maybe. Lover, definitely yes. "This isn't the best time to go into it."

He didn't know if there would be a right time for that.

Two car doors slammed.

"They're here," he said.

Jane reached over and straightened his tie. The gesture surprised him, but seemed so familiar, so natural coming from her, that he felt at peace.

"There," she said. "Now you look like you stepped off the page of a magazine."

"Geek Planet?" he asked.

"Try Hottie World."

"Then you must be in there, too." Her laughter made him smile. "Nervous?"

"A little."

"You'll do fine."

They greeted the man and woman walking toward them.

"Hello, I'm Tiffany Trimble." The reporter, a perky brunette with a dimpled grin and button nose, looked like a bohemian teenager with her long skirt, multiple tank tops and heavy boots, but she'd been with the *Willamette Journal* for years and Chase wasn't about to underestimate her. She handed them each a business card. "Thank you for having us over today. This is our photographer, Saul Mattingly."

Saul shook hands. "I'll be heading over to take pictures of Emma later. I've had better luck photographing kids in their natural environments."

With the pleasantries exchanged, Tiffany asked for a tour of the estate. Saul photographed them walking in the garden. Jane seemed at ease. Her self-confidence over-flowed. She held her head high and her smile remained steady. She showed no outward signs of nervousness. Nothing to suggest she hadn't done this a hundred times. Chase couldn't be prouder of her.

Saul sat them on a bench near the rose arbor. Jane shared an amused glance with Chase. Laughter danced in her eyes. She was enjoying herself, and he liked seeing her so happy.

"Those are going to be some great shots," Tiffany said.

Chase agreed. He wondered if Saul would give him copies.

When they reached the winery, the photograper posi-tioned them in front of the barrels holding wine bottles. The scent of vanilla—Jane's lotion or shampoo—filled Chase's nostrils. He longed to touch her, kiss her. Not the smartest moves in front of the media. But his gaze kept straying to Jane. He struggled to remain focused, in control.

At the barn, Saul snapped more pictures of them standing outside the big double wooden doors. Some playful, others more serious. Chase couldn't keep his eyes off Jane. Every move she made, every expression on her face drew him in. Damn. The situation was fast becoming impossible.

Tiffany wrote in her notebook. "The two of you look good together."

The innuendo was clear, but didn't deserve a comment. He could only imagine how good they looked together. Once other people saw the pictures, would they think so, too? He would take heat from his family, no doubt. But the last thing Jane needed was to be romantically linked to him, to be the subject of gossip. His collar tightened until it threatened to strangle him.

"I've got the shots I wanted," Saul said. "Thanks." With that, the photographer left.

"Why don't we go into the main house?" Chase suggested. "We can sit in the living room."

He led them inside. The housekeeper had left tea and coffee on the table for them.

"Lovely estate." Tiffany sat on a Provençal-style chair. "How did you decide to use the winery for Emma's benefit?"

"When I approached Chase about sponsoring the benefit, he offered to host the event here," Jane said.

The reporter leaned toward her. "So you approached him?"

"Yes."

"Why him?" Tiffany asked. "Why Chase Ryder?"

"First, he's known for being generous to charities. Second, he's rich." Jane grinned. "What more could you hope to find in a sponsor?"

With a chuckle, Tiffany wrote in her notebook and gave him the once-over. "Not much else. You're right about that."

"I feel fortunate Jane approached me," he added. "She has so many ideas that organizing the event has been easy."

Tiffany furrowed her brows. "No obstacles or road-blocks?"

"Nothing major," Jane said. "A few disagreements along the way."

And a few kisses and complications. Not to mention his acting like a fool over a woman he couldn't possibly be with. Chase had to stop the madness. He wasn't the right guy for Jane. His obsessing over her or worse, his being with her would only end in disaster.

Time flew as they answered questions. He didn't know Jane's major in college, but she should consider public relations. The woman was a natural with the media.

"So, Chase," Tiffany said. "This is a different kind of event for you, isn't it?"

"Yes," he said. "In the past, I've been a hands-off contributor. But being a part of Emma's Once Upon A Time benefit has been truly fulfilling. I'd like to do more events like it."

"And would you like to work together again?"

"I've enjoyed working with Jane on the event," he answered without missing a beat. Tiffany was fishing for something, but he wasn't taking the bait. "Our strengths complement each other."

"What about working outside the event?" Tiffany asked. "Has Robin Hood finally met his Maid Marian?"

Damn. He'd been snared and reeled in with one cast. Chase laughed, but inside he seethed. He hadn't expected this kind of question from the reporter. The same kind of questions his family had been inundating him with for the past month. He hadn't known how to answer them, let alone Tiffany.

One thing was clear. He cared about Jane. Today only reaffirmed what he'd felt at the clinic, and then some. But he couldn't make the type of commitment he knew she needed in her life. Jane might be his dream of a wife and mother, but as a husband and father, he came up short at best.

Besides, he wasn't ready to be a couple, to have their relationship publicized and have it printed in black and white. He wasn't ready to say no to bachelorhood. He didn't know if he would ever be ready for that.

"Time will tell, Tiffany." Chase forced a smile. "But a guy's gotta be careful when the only reason a woman approached him in the first place was for his money."

The reporter laughed at his lighthearted comment, and scribbled in her notebook. "And is that the big attraction, Jane? His money?"

She hesitated before she, too, smiled. "Well, it's such a lot of money."

Chase laughed along with them, but he wasn't amused. What had he expected? That she'd tell the reporter and the world she loved him for his mind? For his good heart?

That wasn't what he wanted. It wasn't even true.

"Actually," Jane said, "at first I only wanted him as a sponsor, but Chase has brought so much to the event, proving he isn't only a wallet. Emma and her mother, Michelle and I feel blessed to have met Chase and to have him so involved in this benefit. He's become Emma's fairy godfather, her uncle Chase, and we're so grateful for all he's done."

Humor and the affection filled Jane's voice, but those didn't matter. She needed money. Not only for the benefit, but also for her own future. He had the resources to turn her dream into reality, to allow her to create the perfect life for herself.

He barely heard the final questions from the interviewer. She's not interested in your money, a voice cried inside him. Chase ignored it. Things between them were getting too comfortable, too heated, too…complicated. It would only end in disappointment, and Jane had experienced too much of that in the past. His money could remove the burdens and struggles from her life. Better, it offered him an out. An excuse.

Yes, that's all this really was. An excuse.

But, Chase realized, it was enough.

He wanted out. Now. Before it was too late.

The knock on the door startled Jane. She set her *Legal Environment of Business* textbook down and checked the clock. Nearly ten at night. She hurried to the door before another knock woke Michelle and Emma.

Jane peered through the peephole. Chase. He'd been busy since the interview and seeing him here pleased her. She unlocked and opened the door. "What are you doing here?"

"These are for you, Michelle and Emma for the benefit." He held three big silver Nordstrom boxes, each with a card and a colorful bow. "Open them when you are all together."

She took the packages from Chase and had a good look at him. He wore black pants, a turtleneck and a wool jacket. A little more dressy than normal, but she liked the outfit.

"Thanks." Jane placed the boxes on the floor, but she didn't understand why he delivered the packages tonight when the benefit wasn't until Friday. Unless he had another reason for visiting. Such as seeing her. She smoothed her hair. "Would you like to come in?"

He hung back on the landing.

"Or not," she said.

As he walked inside, she noticed a manila folder shoved under his arm. Something for the benefit? He sat on the couch, but didn't remove his coat.

Maybe he had go back to the office. Jane sat next to

him, wanting to make the most of their time together. "So what's been going on? How's that merger deal?"

He didn't look at her. "Fine."

"So things have improved?"

"Yes."

Only one word answers. He seemed a million miles away. "Are you okay?" She touched his shoulder. He shrugged away. The action felt like a slap. "Chase?"

"Sorry. It's not you. It's me."

She'd heard that before. His words aroused old fears. She fought against the uncertainty threatening to take hold. "What are you talking about?"

As he stared at the folder in his hands, she became more uncomfortable with each passing second. Finally he looked up.

"I want to do something for you, Jane."

His words surprised, but pleased her. Maybe she should stop analyzing everything he said or did. "You brought me a pretty package. I don't need anything else."

"Yes, you do." The softness in his voice contradicted his stiff posture. "I'm giving you a scholarship so you can finish your degree. You won't have to worry about coordinating your class schedule with your work hours. You'll have a living stipend and health insurance."

Shock rippled through Jane. The sudden change in him unnerved her. "I—I don't know what to say."

"Say yes." He handed her three pieces of paper. "The first one describes an endowed scholarship I've established for you. The second is a guarantee to purchase the Hearth, or whatever coffee house you choose, in your name once you've graduated with your degree. The third is a preliminary document for a nonprofit fund for helping cancer patients that will be established in your father's name."

"What do you mean?" She scanned the papers. "What is all of this?"

"Your dreams, Jane," Chase said. "I'm giving you all your dreams. I'm also going to get Michelle a job at Cyberworx. She will have full benefits, including health insurance. And she won't ever have to miss another one of Emma's appointments."

No wonder he'd been acting so strange. He must have been nervous about all of this.

A huge weight lifted from Jane, and her heart felt featherlight. She couldn't imagine the amount of effort it took to make all these arrangements. That he cared to do this filled her with hope. His gift told her how much she meant to him and it was her turn to be honest with him.

"You wanting to do this means so much to me, but I don't need any of these things."

"Jane—"

"Let me finish please." He'd given her the courage to speak from her heart. "Until I met you I didn't believe in anything. Not in other people. Not even myself. I'd stopped living, stopped taking risks, stopped believing. You changed that, Chase. You helped change me. I tried to fight what was happening between us, tried to stand back and ignore it, but I don't want to do that anymore. You're part of my dreams now. You're all I need."

An image of a castle appeared in her mind. The glass slipper fit. She'd found her own Cinderella tale. Her own Prince Charming, a sweet, generous man who loved and believed in her. And her own happily ever after.

Jane hugged Chase. She expected his arms to wrap

around her, but instead he backed away. She slumped against the couch, bewildered. "What is going on?"

"I…can't."

"Can't what?"

"Once the benefit is over, I can't see you anymore Jane. I can't give you what you want."

The castle walls crashed down on her. Emotions choked her. Her mind reeled. "I—I don't understand. You said you were giving me my dreams."

"I am. I don't want to see you struggle. I want you to be happy."

"I'm happy with you," she said.

He stood and walked to the television, avoiding her eyes. And that's when a horrible thought hit her. He wasn't happy with her. He didn't return her feelings.

She let the realization sink in. And then she threw it away.

Jane knew in her heart Chase's disinterest couldn't be true. She'd seen the way he looked at her, held her in his arms, kissed her. This was something else.

"If you want me to be happy, why are you telling me we can't be together?"

"Jane, I won't deny the physical attraction between us. We both know it's there. But I was wrong to kiss you, to give you false hopes. I see you're getting serious, misunderstanding my feelings for you, our friendship. You wouldn't be the first woman to do so. Money is a powerful inducement."

What he was saying was so absurd she laughed. "You think I'm after your money? Me?"

"It doesn't matter. Our having a relationship isn't going to happen. But that doesn't mean you can't finish school without having to juggle your work and class schedules.

And run your own business once you're finished. And have all your dreams come true. You've earned this. You really have."

"So this is my payoff?" She rose. "Is that what you're saying?"

"It's a gift," he said. "My gift to you."

"Gifts don't come with strings." Her temper flared. "I'm not going to accept a bribe so you can ease your conscience, Chase."

A vein twitched on his neck. "That's your choice."

Her choice? Suddenly Jane understood. She raised her chin and boldly met his eyes. "No. You're trying to make this about me. My needs. My choice. But it's really about you. You're a chicken."

"What?"

"You're scared of what's happening between us."

"I'm not scared."

"You're scared." Everything seemed so clear to her. "I'm scared, too. But at least I'm willing to admit my feelings, to face my fears and go for what I want. Not pretend I don't care and try to buy people off or run away."

"That's not what I'm doing."

"I don't believe you." She shoved the papers at him. "I don't want your pity or your handouts or whatever you think buying me off will bring. You can't try to fulfill my dreams without making yourself a part of them, Chase. I know what I want. And I'm not going to settle for anything less."

She'd called him a chicken.

Chase had offered her what anyone else would have considered a magnanimous, incredible gift. But not Jane

Dawson. She'd turned everything down. No, she'd thrown it back in his face and claimed he was scared. Unbelieveable.

He'd been right to believe she'd grown too fond of him. Jane admitting he was part of her dreams and that she wanted him to be part of her future had him almost changing his mind. She sounded so sincere and the…fondness in her eyes when she looked at him had filled him with…

No.

He'd forced himself to be strong and not give in to something that would never last. He'd acted out of practicality, not fear. He'd tried to be kind and generous, and look where that got him. Nowhere.

The day of Emma's benefit, he walked the length of his office. He wasn't pacing. He just needed to do something to get his concentration back. So much of his life had been focused on the fundraiser in the last weeks. And on Jane.

He remembered the anger in her eyes and the way she shoved the papers at him the other night. Too bad he remembered other things, too, like how she'd pressed against him when he'd kissed her on the street, or how she'd laughed with the wind blowing her hair at the picnic.

Chase had no idea how tonight at the benefit would turn out. But once the event was over, he wouldn't have to see or think about Jane Dawson again.

A knock sounded and he was thankful for the distraction.

Amanda hurried into his office. "Michelle Taylor is on line two. She said it was important, an emergency."

Emma. Or Jane.

His heart slammed against his chest. He grabbed the phone and hit the blinking line two button. "Michelle?"

"I'm so sorry to bother you." She spoke in a hushed tone. "We're at the clinic and Emma wanted to talk to you."

Emma, not Jane. The knowledge brought little relief. He plopped into his chair. "Is anything wrong?"

"Emma's red blood cells bottomed out. She's getting a transfusion and I'm...I'm worried the leukemia may be back."

Chase remembered the horrified look on Jane's face when she'd mentioned the word relapse. "But it's not certain."

"No, not..." Michelle's voice wavered. "I got a call from the preschool. Emma was so tired. She fell asleep the minute I got her in the car and she looked so pale. I called the doctor and they had me bring her in. They checked her counts. She needed a blood transfusion, but they also saw something strange in her blood tests. They want to do additional testing to see if there's anything to be concerned about."

"You're at the clinic?"

"Yes. We've been here a while." Michelle's voice cracked. "I know you're busy but Emma wanted to talk to her uncle Chase so I thought I'd call."

A visegrip tightened around his heart. "Put her on."

"I can't right now. She's in the exam room with a nurse," Michelle explained. "I was hoping in few minutes or later...if you don't mind...you could call back."

"Have you talked to Jane about what's going on?"

"No, the doctor said this might be nothing. Emma's needed transfusions before," Michelle explained. "And I don't want Jane to worry. She went through so many ups-and-downs with her father and with the dessert in a few hours, I want to spare her as much as I can. Though I'll need to get word to her about tonight."

"I'll take care of it," he offered. "But you know Jane would want to be with you."

"Yes, but it's not necessary." Michelle released a sigh. "Jane's a lot stronger than me, a lot stronger than she realizes. I've relied a little bit too much on her this past year and that hasn't been fair to her."

He'd tried to be fair to her. She hadn't wanted that. "She cares about you and Emma."

"I know," Michelle said. "But Jane's struggled so much. She should concentrate on her own future, not focus so much on us. That's going to make it harder if Emma—"

"Don't think about any ifs."

Michelle sniffled. "I'm trying."

"Good." He was a poor substitute for Jane, but he'd do his best to support Michelle. "I'll be right there."

"No, no. I just thought…if you wouldn't mind calling Emma back…"

"But I do mind," he said. "I want to be there."

A beat passed. "Are you sure?"

"Yes." Chase hung up the telephone. He ran through what he had to do, but one thought kept him sitting at his desk.

Jane.

He understood Michelle's reasoning, but he also knew she needed Jane. Chase felt torn.

"What can I do, boss?" Amanda asked.

His assistant's voice, full of concern, spurred him into action. He jotted down a list of what needed to be done for the benefit tonight. He handed the list to Amanda.

"Call Sam and my family." Chase glanced at his watch, wishing he could transport himself to Emma's doctor's office. That was the kind of technology he needed right now. "Everyone's going to have to help out tonight."

"Don't worry, we can handle it."

"Find me a couple of magazines. The kind a mom might want to read." He scratched his chin. "And whatever you do, don't let Jane know anything is wrong with Emma. Tell her that Michelle and Emma are running late. I'll take care of the rest."

Somehow.

And if the news was bad…no, he wouldn't go there.

Amanda's eyes clouded. "Is Emma going to be okay?"

"I don't know, Amanda," Chase admitted, his gut tied up in knots. "I really don't know."

CHAPTER ELEVEN

STANDING next to the wishing well, Jane surveyed the room. Over two hundred and fifty wineglasses sat on a table behind the check-in area, colorful, aromatic blossoms surrounded the candles in each of the Cinderella carriage centerpieces, a gold throne sat on the elevated and twinkling white lights hung from the walls and ceiling. The transformation to fairy-tale land was complete.

She'd done it.

Emma was going to love the dessert. Michelle, too. And that made everything worth it.

Including Jane's broken heart.

Tears stung her eyes. She blinked them away. She was not going to let her blighted romance ruin Emma's special night.

Jane hadn't been able to help her father or herself, but she could help Michelle and Emma. That counted for something. Okay, a lot. The fundraiser had kept Jane going these past few days. She'd thrown her heart and soul into making the benefit a success. She wasn't going to allow her feelings and frustration about Chase to get in the way.

He would be here any minute.

Jane took a deep breath and tried to prepare herself.

She could be professional. She could pretend his kisses

hadn't curled her toes. She could pretend she hadn't dreamed of a future with him and hadn't embarrassed herself, confessing her feelings to someone who didn't know how to return them.

She wouldn't think about how he'd thrown away what they had, what they could have had, because he was afraid. How he'd tried to buy her off because doing so was easier than investing his heart and energy into a relationship.

She would do it because she had no other choice.

With her resolve locked into place, Jane straightened the stack of white cards and aligned the gel pens for guests to use to write wishes for Emma. She wanted to be the first one. She wrote with a purple pen:

> My dearest Princess Emma,
> I can't wait to watch you grow and see you live happily ever after. I love you, Jelly Bean.
> Jane
> xoxo

She kissed the card and tossed it into the wishing well.

Jane took her bag into the ladies' room. She pulled off her jeans and T-shirt and slipped into a stunning green cocktail dress—a present from Chase. The three boxes he'd brought that night contained party outfits for her, Emma and Michelle, perfectly sized. Jane had considered tossing hers into the trash, but decided the dress was nothing but a party decoration, like the fairy lights, the flowers and rented tablecloths. And like the linens, the dress was going back tomorrow.

She put on make-up, added her mother's locket and earrings and stared at her reflection in the mirror.

You are so beautiful.

She remembered Chase's words. Let them take root. She wasn't the person she used to be. It was time to say goodbye to plain Jane once and for all.

Out in the main room, she double-checked her To-do list. Michelle and Emma wouldn't be arriving until the event started. The only thing missing—Chase.

He'd sent her an e-mail after their argument saying nothing had changed with the benefit. No matter what had happened between them, he'd promised her that. Michelle and Emma, too. He wouldn't let them down the way others had done in the past. As angry as she'd been with him, his keeping his word meant a lot.

So where could he be?

Anticipation filled the air. Uniformed servers hurried back and forth from the bustling kitchen. Volunteers readied themselves for the arrival of the guests.

"Where is the extra ice?" a bartender asked.

As she directed him to the freezer, Chase's brother-in-law Sam walked in carrying a cardboard box.

"You look great, Jane." He didn't look so bad himself in a dark suit, blue shirt and gold silk tie. "And this place is absolutely amazing. Fantastic job."

"Thanks," she said. "What do you have there?"

"Chase wanted me to bring the programs for tonight."

"Where is he?" she asked, trying to sound nonchalant.

The look of pity in Sam's eyes told her everything she needed to know. Chase wasn't coming. The knowledge twisted like a knife inside her. She couldn't breathe.

"He'll be here when he can," Sam explained. "In the meantime, tell me what I should be doing."

His words hardly registered. Jane thought her heart

couldn't be hurt anymore. She'd been wrong. She handed him a clipboard with Chase's To-do list.

"I can do this," Sam said, reading it. "Piper and the rest of our family will be here soon to help, too."

"Okay. Thanks." But it wasn't okay. Jane gritted her teeth. This wasn't only about raising money for Emma's medical treatments. This was making her feel loved and supported. She needed those things as badly. Chase Ryder couldn't buy off or delegate his emotional obligations to Emma.

No matter how hard he tried.

Some blame lay with Jane. She should have never made him a part of Michelle and Emma's lives. Chase claimed he'd changed. That he wanted to do more than write checks. That he wanted to be involved. That he wanted to help. She had believed him, trusted him, loved him. And as a consequence, little Emma had lost her heart to him…just as Jane had.

And that made it worse.

Because he wasn't here. He hadn't changed. He wouldn't change.

Once again she was on her own. Only this time, Jane realized, that was okay. She could handle tonight by herself.

And she would.

Chase knew better than to speed. Getting pulled over by the police would only delay him. But driving within the posted limits wasn't easy. Emma needed him.

At the clinic, Rachel, the nurse, led him to an exam room. Michelle sat on the edge of the bed where a sleeping Emma lay under a blanket. She was hooked up to tubes and receiving a blood transfusion.

He placed a gift bag containing a pink rhinestone tiara for Emma on the counter. He had planned on giving the crown to her tonight at the benefit, but now seemed a better time.

"Thanks for coming, Chase." Michelle focused her attention on Emma. "She'll be happy to see you."

He handed Michelle two magazines. A poor distraction, but he'd wanted to bring her something. "What's the latest?"

"They want to do a bone marrow test."

He knew from the DVD they'd put together for tonight the test could help them determine whether or not Emma had relapsed. A cold knot formed in his stomach. "When?"

"I don't know yet."

He watched the rise and fall of the blanket over Emma. Never had he known the relief a simple breath could bring. He clung to the sight of her breathing like a lifeline.

How did Michelle stand this? This wasn't the first time she'd waited for a test, for a diagnosis, for a piece of news, but the uncertainty was driving Chase crazy and he'd only arrived. He wanted to pace, but didn't want to make Michelle nervous. "Do you want me to talk to someone?"

A corner of her mouth lifted. "Thanks, but I doubt even you can make things happen any faster."

He'd give away everything he had if he could. He made a fist. Wanted to punch something. But anger and frustration wouldn't help Michelle and Emma.

"Can I get you anything?" he asked. "Do something to help?"

"You're here," Michelle said, her voice quiet. "That's a big something."

It wasn't enough.

He sat on one of the chairs, but couldn't get comfortable. The dimmed overhead light cast an odd pallor on the room making Michelle seem more vulnerable. He liked having answers and fixing problems, but he was at a loss here. "You okay?"

"I don't know." She chewed on her lower lip. "I knew this was a possibility in the back of my mind, but you don't dwell on it. You can't. It's a worst-case scenario, your most dreaded fear so I didn't go there. I concentrated on the cure rate. On all the positives. You know, like she had the good ALL. Good leukemia. Now that's an oxymoron.

"But thinking about it coming back…" Michelle shivered. "This is a hundred times worse than when I got the original diagnosis. Back then I didn't have a clue about what was ahead of us, but now I do. It would be like starting over and the possibility of losing…"

Chase felt physically ill. He imagined what Jane would say. "We don't know if Emma's relapsed."

Michelle flinched. Damn. He shouldn't have said the word. He needed Jane here. She could handle this better than him.

"You're right," Michelle mumbled. "I know you're right. Dr. Kempler said the same thing. Emma's little body has gotten overwhelmed before and needed a transfusion or something has shown up in a test that turned out to be nothing, but I still worry. I can't help it."

"You're doing great." He stood and patted her shoulder awkwardly. "You're amazing."

"I'm a mom. That's all." She caressed Emma's cheek. "She's such a sweet baby. So innocent. So beautiful. Chase…"

He met Michelle's gaze. It wasn't her tears that punched him in the gut, but the fear in her eyes.

"Emma is all I've got. I can't lose her. I just can't."

"You don't have to," he said. "The tests could show nothing is wrong. Maybe the doctor will have good news. And in the meantime…"

What?

He couldn't promise her anything. He couldn't buy his way out of this one. There wasn't anything he could do.

"…I'm here," he said.

Lame. Very lame.

"Thanks." Michelle wiped her eyes. She took a deep breath and exhaled slowly. "No matter what happens, I've been blessed by every minute Emma has been with me. Nothing, not even cancer, can take that away."

Michelle stared down at her daughter, the love flowing between the two so strong he could almost touch it. He might have everything a guy could ever desire and achieved all he'd set out to accomplish, but he stood here, in the presence of something special, something precious, humbled and feeling more than a little empty inside.

And that's when it hit Chase.

For all his degrees, for all his street smarts, he didn't know anything about the most important thing.

Love.

Jane had been correct. He had been making excuses.

He'd been scared, too scared to love. Of failing at the one thing that mattered most.

He thought about Jane's ex-boyfriend and Michelle's ex-husband. Was that why they gave up so much and just left? Talk about lousy reasoning. But wasn't that what he'd done? Chase rubbed his chin.

He'd never put himself out there. He'd never taken the chance. He'd never even tried.

And if he didn't do something about it fast he was going to lose the one person who mattered most, the one person he wanted a life with. He might have already lost her.

Jane. Caring, giving, beautiful Jane.

She was always there, physically and emotionally, for those she cared about. That's what mattered. Being there. Loving. Chase finally understood.

He only hoped it wasn't too late.

The delighted gasps from the first shuttle load of guests and an anonymous one thousand dollar donation kicked off the event with a bang. Music from a string quartet filled the room. The scent of wine mingled with chocolate. Pride bubbled up inside Jane.

More shuttle vans arrived. Smartly dressed guests entered and checked in with Kendra and the rest of the crew from the Hearth. Zoe and Ally handed each person a wineglass with a personalized nametag on the stem and a boxed chocolate truffle inside the glass. Chase's sisters, Piper and Hannah, and his parents passed out programs. Sam coordinated the multimedia presentation along with Hannah's husband, Grant.

As Jane circled the room, she recognized friends, customers from the Hearth and two of her professors amid the more famous faces. She searched for Emma and Michelle among the crowd, but didn't see them. Someone called her name, and she turned.

"I've been looking for you," Chase's assistant, Amanda, wearing an elegant blue dress, said. "Michelle wanted you to know she's running late."

The news meant Jane could relax. Okay, maybe not relax, but at least she wouldn't have to keep worrying. "Do you know why?"

"I didn't ask."

"Thanks. I hope you enjoy tonight."

Everyone else seemed to be having fun. Guests examined the baskets and items up for bid on the silent auction tables. Others wrote cards for Emma and tossed them into the wishing well. Some tasted goodies and admired the lovely dessert buffet complete with a castle ice sculpture, donated by a friend of the caterer, and a chocolate fondue fountain.

"Great job, Jane," Fred, her usher friend gushed. The CEO from a local sporting goods manufacturer agreed, and the two men talked about the upcoming University of Oregon football game.

Compliment after compliment came her way. She appreciated and accepted each tiny affirmation graciously, but none of them soothed her raw and aching heart. It would be nice to have someone to share her accomplishments with.

But it wouldn't always be like this. Someday, when her heart stopped hurting, she would try loving again. Jane would never settle for less than she wanted for fear of being disappointed. Or being left. At least Chase had given her that.

Cinderella had to go to the ball alone, but she had and was surviving.

Jane would always survive.

An hour into the benefit, Michelle and Emma still hadn't arrived. This was beyond late. Worried, Jane tried calling, but no one answered. They must be on their way, but she couldn't hold off the evening's program any longer.

She climbed the stairs to the small stage they'd constructed, went over to the microphone and stared down at the hundreds of guests gathered in front of her. "Hello, my name is Jane Dawson and on behalf of Chase Ryder and Ryder Estate Winery, I would like to welcome all of you to Once Upon A Time…a benefit for Emma Taylor."

Applause greeted her.

"I'm not quite sure where our guest of honor is—" people laughed "—but I'd like to show you a story about a little princess and her fight against a dragon called Leukemia."

The lights dimmed. Jane signaled Sam to begin the special DVD they'd created for tonight. Before the film could start, the big double doors at the back of the room opened. Distracted by the sound, the audience turned. Jane stared across the crowded room.

Illuminated by the twinkling fairy lights, Chase strode into the barn with Emma perched like a princess in his arms. She wore a sparkling pink rhinestone tiara and purple boa. Michelle followed behind them. All three wore casual clothes. Chase in jeans, a shirt and sports jacket, Emma in pink overalls and lace trimmed blouse and Michelle in the dress she'd put on that morning.

Jane's heart swelled. Her mouth went dry. He was here. They were here. But what was going on?

Chase caught her eye and nodded. She cleared her throat.

"Ladies and gentlemen," Jane announced, more relieved than she could have imagined. "Your host for tonight, Chase Ryder."

He traveled across the floor with athletic grace. Seeing him with Emma in his arms caused Jane to catch her breath. He was really here. He hadn't let Emma down.

Chase joined her in the spotlight in front of the microphone. Her pulse quickened at his closeness. "Thanks, Jane. But tonight isn't about me. It's about two very special people. Emma and Michelle Taylor."

Michelle folded Jane in her arms.

Jane hugged her back. "What is going on?" she whispered.

But Chase was still talking. "That's who you need to hear from tonight. Why don't you say hello to all the people who came to see you tonight, Emma."

"Hello people," Emma said, then giggled.

A chorus of "hellos" rose from the crowd, and Emma practically glowed.

Chase motioned for Michelle to take over the microphone. He placed Emma on the gold garland-bedecked throne setup on the left corner of the stage.

"I'm sorry we're so late," Michelle said. "But one of the things you learn living with leukemia is not to take anything for granted."

Anxious, Jane crossed over to Chase. He squeezed her hand, then tugged her away and off the stage.

Michelle spoke about Emma's cancer, how she had needed a blood transfusion today and would need a bone marrow test on Monday. Tears pricked Jane's eyes. She knew the terror plaguing Michelle at this moment...about her daughter and leukemia. But that didn't stop her. Michelle's voice wavered, tears glistened in her eyes, but she kept going, telling Emma's story. The audience was completely quiet. The catering staff from the kitchen joined the crowd.

As Jane listened to the moving testimony, pride and love for Michelle filled her. No matter what happened with the bone marrow test, her friends would make it. They would get through this in one piece. Jane knew that in her heart.

She glanced up at the tall man beside her. The man who had brought Michelle and Emma to the benefit, who had brought hope and heart break back into Jane's life.

"You came," she said.

"Sometimes the best you can do is show up." His tender gaze met hers. "I understand that now, thanks to you."

Jane couldn't speak, couldn't breathe. She was vaguely aware of applause in the darkness. Her pulse skittered, her body betraying her resolve to remain indifferent to him. She tried to slip her hand from his, but his grip only tightened.

An image of Emma dressed up like a princess appeared on the projection screen behind the stage. Music played and the story, narrated by a local newscaster, began with "Once upon a time…"

As the guests watched the DVD, Emma skipped over, dragging Michelle behind her. Transfusions usually gave Emma an extra boost of energy and made her feel better, and today was no different than the times before.

"Did you see the ice castle and the wishing well and the chocolate?" Emma asked.

"I did." Jane finally tugged her hand free from Chase's warm clasp. Kneeling, she hugged the little girl. "Do you like everything, jelly bean?"

Emma nodded, her curls bouncing wildly. "Thank you, Jane."

"A lot of people helped out."

"Thank you people," Emma said to no one in particular.

Michelle's gaze darted from Jane to Chase. "Come on, princess." Michelle picked up Emma. "Let's check out the dessert table."

Jane watched the two go, feeling her composure leaving with them. Squaring her shoulders, she turned to face Chase.

"Everything is perfect, Jane," Chase said, his low voice filled with respect. "Just like you said it would be."

The intense look in his eyes nearly did her in. Her knees went weak. She hated how after everything, feelings for him remained. He still had a huge chunk of her heart. For how long? She lifted her chin. "I need to check on the silent auction."

"Three minutes," he said. "That's all I need."

She hesitated, torn. She stared at the twinkling lights. Yes, he'd come. He'd been there for Emma. Despite the heartache he'd caused her, he was a good man. But she wasn't certain she wanted to hear what he had to say. Except that she remembered that he'd given her his time when they first met and she asked to speak with him. She could do the same. She owed him that much.

"Three minutes," she agreed.

But for several seconds he was silent, as if he didn't know where to begin.

She decided to have pity on him. "Thank you for coming. Thank you for bringing Emma."

He shook his head. "It's about time I showed up."

She frowned, puzzled. "You couldn't before. The transfusion—"

"That's not what I meant. You always show up," he explained. "For your father, Michelle, Emma, the benefit, your own life, me. I've never done that. I wrote checks, did everything so I wouldn't have to be there. Even with you, I might have been there physically, but not mentally. Not emotionally."

Chase gave her another one of those long, intense looks, and her chest tightened. No. She couldn't give in, but she couldn't walk away, either.

"You might not have been much of a risk-taker in the past, Jane, but when it comes to the people you care about, you don't hold back. I respect that. You." He took her hand in his again. "The first time I met you, I thought you needed rescuing. Especially after I met Michelle and Emma. But I was wrong. So very wrong. You were the one who had everything under control. You are strong, so giving, so nurturing. People can't help but be drawn to you.

"I know I was, and that scared me. I might be known for taking risks. I've risked my fortune, my business, my life, but I realized today I've never risked the most important thing."

She could barely breathe. "What's that?"

"My heart. I've never put my heart on the line for love."

His words melted her resolve. Who was she kidding? It lay in a puddle on the floor. Hope filled her.

"You were right," he said. "I've been too scared to risk my heart. Afraid to depend on anyone. Afraid to have them count on me too much, or too little. Afraid to let that person in, when I could get hurt, betrayed. Afraid to love."

Maybe it was possible... She wanted to believe desperately.

"I convinced myself I didn't need a woman in my life, that I didn't need love. But when I saw Michelle and Emma today. Something happened. I realized how much I was missing out on. How much I would lose with you not in my life."

Jane's heart jolted. His words echoed her feelings.

"I need you. I need you to be here and rescue me from my loveless life." Uncertainty crept into his expression. "Will you, Jane? Will you rescue me?"

Hope gave way to joy. She inhaled.

"If you need time, I understand." Chase didn't take his eyes off her. He continued holding her hand in his strong, steady grasp. "I made a big mistake. I hurt you. I know that. And I'm sorry. But I won't do it again. I'll never not be there for you again."

"It's okay." She reached up and brushed her lips across his. "We're both experts at shutting ourselves off from love, at playing it safe. But, Chase, you taught me a great deal, too. I never believed I was capable of doing so much, but you always did. You made me feel important and respected."

He caressed her cheek. "You did that yourself, my love."

My love. She could get used to hearing that.

"I didn't believe in being rescued myself, or counting on anyone to save me. But I do now, and you have." She touched his shoulder, knowing she could always rely on him. "With you I felt secure for the first time in my life. I learned to trust. You made me believe in fairy tales again."

A flash of mischief crossed his face. "As in Prince Charming?"

She shrugged. "To be honest, I'm a bit partial to your nibbling shark side."

"Whatever you desire, milady."

"I desire not to play it safe ever again. I'd be happy to rescue you. To be there for you. Today, tomorrow, always. After all you've done for me, it's the least I can do. But you have to promise to do the same for me. Deal?"

"Deal." He pulled something red from his jacket pocket.

A feather boa. He placed it around her neck and pulled her in close. "I love you, Jane Dawson."

"I love you, Chase Ryder."

His arm slipped around her. She felt giddy and free, like she was dancing without moving her feet.

"Will you marry me and live happily ever after?" he asked.

It was the last thing she expected to hear. Sure, they loved each other, but they hardly knew each other. They came from different worlds and—

"Jane?" he asked.

She realized she was still being too cautious. No need for that. No need at all. Jane rose on her tiptoes and kissed him firmly on the lips. As she melted into his warmth and his strength, she was back where she belonged—home. Someone whistled, another person cheered. She drew away.

"I just needed a minute." Jane ran her fingers through Chase's curls and gazed into his intoxicating blue eyes, eyes that saw only her. "Taking big risks requires a little practice."

"Practice all you want, but right now could you make me the happiest man on Earth and say yes?" he asked.

Joy bubbled inside her. "Yes, I will marry you."

"Yes." He looked out at the crowd around them. "She said yes."

"Finally." Amanda handed glasses of wine to them. "A toast to my boss' good sense. And Jane's, too."

"I knew it would happen to you one day, Chase." Sam raised his own glass, one arm around Piper, who laughed.

Jane laughed, too, and rested her head against Chase's shoulder. She felt the beating of his heart. She had never dared to believe in fairy tales. But she did now, and she wanted it all. Love. Marriage. A happy ending.

And she wanted them all with Chase.

EPILOGUE

One and a half years later

THE flashbulbs nearly blinded her, but Jane's confident steps carried her across the stage, her heart so full and light she thought she might float.

"Jane Dawson Ryder. Bachelor of Arts with Honors."

The beaming dean of undergraduate studies shook her hand. "Congratulations on a new beginning. Both of your new beginnings," he added with a twinkle.

She touched her heavily rounded stomach, visible beneath her black academic gown with one hand, and clutched her diploma box with the other. "Thank you so much."

Jane made her way to the steps leading from the stage and reached for the metal handrail. But Chase was waiting for her, ahead of the ushers to help her down, his strong hand firm under her elbow.

"Congratulations, my love." His smile crinkled the corners of his eyes. "I'm so proud of you."

She gazed at his handsome face. "I love you."

Their kiss knocked the mortarboard from her head.

As Chase stooped to retrieve it, Jane could see into the

stands behind him. Her entire family sat in the audience. Sam and Grant videotaped the graduation ceremony while Piper and Hannah kept their children seated and entertained. Michelle and Chase's mother snapped pictures. Emma sat on Chase's father's lap.

Emma hadn't relapsed, but remained in remission. She'd completed her treatment and was feeling great.

"Everyone's here," Jane said.

"They wouldn't miss it for the world. They love you. And so do I." Chase put his arm around her—no easy feat since she was approximately the size of a house—and grinned. "You can always count on us to show up whether you want us to or not."

She touched the locket around her neck and imagined her mother's and father's smiling faces inside.

Jane had been given precious gifts. Chase, a child, a new family. She was living a dream and taking each day with the hope of tomorrow. And most of all she was enjoying every single minute. Happily ever after didn't get much better than this.

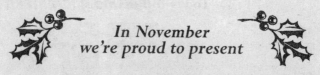

REQUEST YOUR FREE BOOKS!

2 FREE NOVELS PLUS 2 FREE GIFTS!

SILHOUETTE
Romance®

From Today to Forever...

COMING NEXT MONTH

#1842 A VOW TO KEEP—Cara Colter
Rick Chase found himself promising to step back temporarily
into his old friend Linda Starr's life to help her out. But then he
met the woman she'd become—a woman with spirit, passion and
unmatched beauty! Promises could be troublesome. They demanded
more than he wanted to give, but had the potential to reward him
with more than he'd ever imagined!

#1843 BLIND-DATE MARRIAGE—Fiona Harper
Serena loves everything in life, except for blind dates! She's turned
her back on her unconventional upbringing, and her deepest wish is
to find the man to spend the rest of her life with…. Jake is a highly
successful and focused businessman. He's worked hard to escape
his roots, and now lives by one rule: *never* get married!

#1844 MILLIONAIRE DAD: WIFE NEEDED—
Natasha Oakley
Nick Regan-Phillips is a millionaire, and the world assumes he has
it all. But he's got a secret. He's a single dad, his daughter, Rosie, is
deaf and he's struggling to communicate with her. Lydia Stanford
is a beautiful award-winning journalist—and seemingly the only
person who can help Nick forge a bond with his daughter.

#1845 A MOTHER FOR HIS DAUGHTER—Ally Blake
How To Marry a Billionaire
Just as Gracie had run out of money and was about to book her
flight home to Australia she'd been rescued! A gorgeous Italian had
hired her to live in his magnificent Tuscan home and be nanny to
his little girl! Luca was thrilled—the new nanny had brought smiles
and laughter back into his daughter's life. He wanted Gracie to stay
forever—as his wife….

SRCNM1106